# I WILL FIND THE KEY

Alex Ahndoril is a new pseudonym for the writers behind Lars Kepler, Alexandra and Alexander Ahndoril. Lars Kepler is a No.1 bestselling international sensation, whose Killer Instinct thrillers have sold more than 17 million copies in 40 languages.

# I WILL FIND THE KEY

ALEX AHNDORIL

ZAFFRE

Originally published in Sweden by Albert Bonniers Förlag in 2023
This edition published in the UK in 2024 by
ZAFFRE
An imprint of Zaffre Publishing Group
A Bonnier Books UK Company
4th Floor, Victoria House, Bloomsbury Square, London, WC1B 4DA
Owned by Bonnier Books
Sveavägen 56, Stockholm, Sweden

Copyright © Alex Ahndoril, 2024

Published by agreement with Salomonsson Agency

Translation copyright © 2024 by Alice Menzies

All rights reserved.
No part of this publication may be reproduced,
stored or transmitted in any form by any means, electronic,
mechanical, photocopying or otherwise, without the
prior written permission of the publisher.

The right of Alex Ahndoril to be identified as Author of this
work has been asserted by them in accordance with the
Copyright, Designs and Patents Act, 1988.

This is a work of fiction. References to real people, events,
establishments, organisations, or locales are intended only to
provide a sense of authenticity and are used fictitiously. All other
characters, and all incidents and dialogue, are drawn from the
author's imagination and are not to be construed as real.

A CIP catalogue record for this book is
available from the British Library.

Hardback ISBN: 978-1-80418-728-9
Trade paperback ISBN: 978-1-80418-729-6

*Also available as an ebook and an audiobook*

1 3 5 7 9 10 8 6 4 2

Typeset by IDSUK (Data Connection) Ltd
Printed and bound in Great Britain by Clays Ltd, Elcograf S.p.A.

Zaffre is an imprint of Zaffre Publishing Group
A Bonnier Books UK company
www.bonnierbooks.co.uk

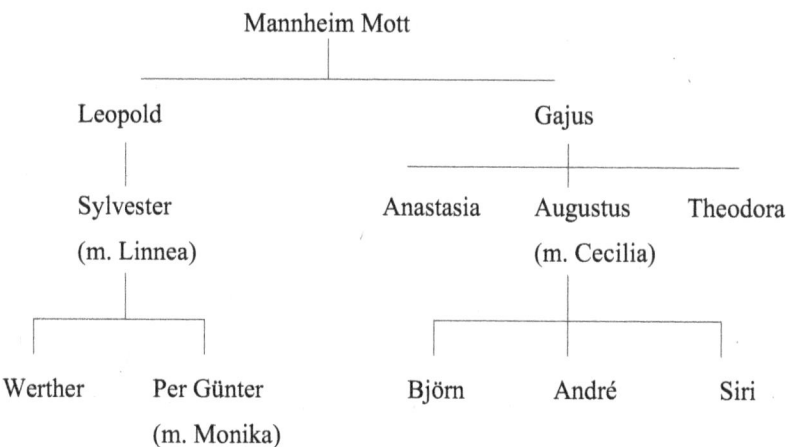

*The passengers and crew of a Lufthansa flight from Ankara to Hamburg are feared dead following a plane crash in Romania. The Boeing 747, carrying three hundred and sixty-two passengers, lost altitude thirty minutes after take-off and came down close to the Bicaz Gorge in the north-east of the country. A spokesperson from the Ministry for Foreign Affairs has said there were five Swedish citizens on board.*

# 1

As she ate a late solo lunch in the August sun, Julia had no idea that she was about to come face to face with a mystery that would demand the very utmost of her, a case she may not be able to solve on her own.

She was sitting at one of the tables outside the market hall in Östermalm. An electric scooter had been dumped on the litter-strewn ground nearby, and it emitted a shrill beep at regular intervals.

Every morning, once Julia had finished her make-up, she liked to lean in to the mirror and say a quiet hello to her mother. She had inherited her fair brows and sad, dark green eyes. Her full lips and her straight nose. And when the sun hit her hair, it shimmered with a coppery tone.

It had been her thirty-third birthday last week, which meant she had finally passed her mother in age. She had taken the day off work and spent it curled up in bed, reading an American paper on bloodstain pattern analysis with the curtains closed. In one of the case studies, a single bullet had split in two upon impact with a rib, causing two exit wounds.

Julia had let the delivery driver leave the flowers from Sidney outside her apartment, waiting until she heard the door to the street swing shut before she went out to get them.

Twenty-five red roses, year after year.

That had cheered her up slightly, but she had forced herself not to answer the phone when Sidney called that evening. She didn't want to start crying, to ask him to come over, because she knew he would.

He would come over and comfort her, the way he always did, but it was unsustainable to keep begging for his pity. That wasn't what she needed from him, and finally acknowledging that was her real birthday present to herself.

She had a plan now. A goal.

Julia knew that she would never be able to win back Sidney's love, but she had a clear vision of a future in which they worked together, ate lunch together and sat up late into the night, discussing every case in detail together.

A homeless man pushing an overloaded shopping trolley crashed into a scaffolding pole and started muttering to himself, gesturing anxiously.

Julia tucked a stray lock of hair behind her ear and turned her attention back to her food, though she was already pretty full. She had ordered steamed turbot with hollandaise sauce, white asparagus and finely-chopped capers. The sun filtered through her glass of chilled Sancerre wine, painting a pale shadow on the table in front of her.

A plane soared overhead, making its way across Stockholm.

Julia lowered her cutlery and discreetly covered her ears until the roar had passed, stopping herself from looking up at the white vapour trails.

She waited a moment, sighed at her own behaviour and then took out her phone to check her schedule for the week. Follow-up meetings and a safety briefing with the Division of Space and Plasma Physics at the Royal Institute of Technology.

Two men in their thirties had sat down at the next table, both in slim-fitting suits and polished shoes, and from the corner of her eye Julia noticed one of them trying to catch her attention. She dropped her phone back into her bag and beckoned to the waiter. As she paid, she happened to meet the man's pale blue eyes. He held her gaze, giving her such a playful, flirty smile that she couldn't help but return the gesture.

Julia reached for her silvery cane, which was leaning against the other chair, and used it to get up. The man blushed and turned away.

She left her table, cutting across the square towards Storgatan.

There were certain angles from which she was attractive, and she had lost count of the number of times men had started to flirt with her only to lose interest as the light shifted or the wind blew her hair back from her cheek. Julia often joked about those moments, but deep down she always hoped the next man would react differently when he noticed her cane or the scar on her face.

She was still young, after all. She needed to fall in love again.

After pausing briefly to compose herself in the shade outside the church, she forced herself to keep going, not stopping until she reached Styrmansgatan 15. The brass plate on the door read *Stark Detective Agency*.

Julia leaned her specially adapted cane against the wall. It was made from titanium alloy, with an ergonomic grip and a black rubber foot. She dug out her keys, unlocked the door and made her way inside. After disabling the alarm, she looked up at the mirror. Her scar looked like it had been drawn in white pen, a vertical line across one side of her face, stretching from her forehead to the very edge of her right eyebrow and down to her jaw.

The cool air in the office smelled like old wood, books and leather.

Julia dumped her bag on the desk, opened the windows onto the lush inner courtyard and went through to the kitchen to make herself a double espresso.

She had been Julia Mendelson during the seven years she was married to Sidney, but since the divorce she had taken her father's surname again, Stark – a name that could be traced all the way back to their ancestor, the soldier Lars Stark, born in 1761.

In the void after Sid, overcome by the sense that her entire life had been a mistake, Julia had decided to quit her job as a clerk at Stockholm District Court. Her time at the courthouse had taught her that she had a knack for reading people, and with each trial she sat through, her frustration with the courts' failure to unearth the truth had grown and grown. She always knew exactly what had happened and why, but the role of clerk didn't allow her to stand up and share that knowledge with the room.

In addition to her logical mind, something she had worked hard to develop over the years, Julia had the ability to deploy an extreme focus in certain moments. Whenever that happened, it was as though time ground to a halt – the way it does in the face of death – and she was able to pick up on details and expressions that most others missed. There was nothing supernatural about her abilities, of course; it was simply another part of her trauma, her mental fragility.

Years ago, long before she ever met Sid, her entire world had come crashing down, shattering like a wine glass hitting a stone floor. And as she put the pieces back together, everything had changed – most things for the worse, but not all. That was what she told herself, anyway, though perhaps that was simply an attempt to console herself, to find meaning in the senselessness of it all.

Julia had enjoyed her job as a clerk, but after the divorce she had started to dream about becoming an investigator with the Norrmalm Police, just like Sidney. She knew she would never actually make it into the force, her body was much too complicated for that, and so she had opened her own detective agency instead.

Most of the jobs were simple enough – affairs, background checks, suspected corporate theft – but every now and again a more complex case dropped into her lap, one that required her full analytical abilities.

Julia took her coffee back through to the office and glanced down at her scratched old wristwatch.

A pneumatic drill rattled somewhere in the distance.

She switched on her computer and was just about to sit down when the buzzer rang. Julia glanced at her diary. There were no meetings scheduled, but she grabbed her cane and got up to see who it was.

Standing on the pavement outside was a tall man with white hair. He looked to be in his fifties, wearing a beige trench coat over a navy blazer, a pair of light trousers and brown shoes.

'Ah, hello. My name is Per Günter Mott. I, um, don't have an appointment, but I ... I was hoping ...' He trailed off and rubbed his head with a shaking hand.

'How can I help you?' asked Julia.

'I think I'd like to use your services, if ...'

'Come in, Per Günter.'

'Please, call me PG.'

'You can hang your coat here.'

Julia moved to one side to make space for him. She had real difficulty with all forms of physical contact, and the sensation of skin on skin was enough to give her a panic attack.

The man stepped inside, looked around and then took off his thin coat.

He was slim, with something delicate and boyish about him, as though he hadn't yet realised he was getting older.

Julia showed him through to her office and told him to take a seat on the sofa. His jacket was crumpled at the back, she noticed, perhaps because he had spent several hours in a car or on a train.

'Can I get you something to drink? Tea, coffee, water?'

'I'm fine, thank you.'

'Just let me know if you change your mind.'

Julia noticed his eyes wandering around the room as he steeled himself to say whatever he had come to say.

'Before I get to the matter at hand, I need to know whether this meeting is confidential,' he said, taking a deep breath.

'You have my complete discretion whether you hire me or not.'

'So you aren't allowed to tell anyone what I've said or shown you?'

'No.'

The man's fingers briefly drummed the arm of the sofa.

'Not even the police?'

'Not even the police,' she reassured him.

# 2

Julia reached for a notepad and pen from her desk and then took a seat in the armchair opposite the man. His forehead had started to glisten, and she saw that his hand was shaking as he reached into his inside pocket.

'OK, I'd like you to take a look at this picture,' he said, setting his phone down on the table in front of her.

A wave of anxiety seemed to wash over him as she picked it up and studied the photograph on the screen. It was timestamped 23.25 the previous evening, but there was no metadata to show where the image had been taken. In the bright glare of the flash, a man was slumped back against a brick wall on a bare concrete floor, his hands bound in his lap. His checked shirt had ridden up over his rounded belly, and his trousers were creased around his groin. The man's head was hidden beneath a jute sack, one side of which was drenched in blood. It had spilled down his chest and stomach, between his spread legs, forming a large, dark pool on the floor beneath him. The image was slightly blurry, which made it difficult to tell whether or not the blood had started to coagulate.

'I found this picture on my phone this morning,' PG explained. 'But I don't know how it got there. That's why I'm here. I came straight to see you, I couldn't just sit around with ...'

His voice faltered, and he swallowed hard and wiped the sweat from his upper lip.

'Who is he?' asked Julia.

'I don't know, I didn't want to guess. I really don't understand a thing,' he said, wringing his hands.

'You don't have any idea? This picture was taken around half eleven last night.'

PG's face was pained, pale.

'I'm ... The thing is that I drink sometimes. And when I do, I sometimes end up having a bit too much.'

'OK.'

'So much that I end up with gaps in my memory, hours and hours that just vanish.'

'And that happened last night?'

'Yes. It could be because I took fifty milligrams of Atarax at lunch, which is an idiotic thing to do if you're drinking ... but I just can't stand our shareholder meetings otherwise,' PG explained, rubbing his cheek with his knuckles. 'In any case ... as you might understand, I'm worried that I may have hurt this man.'

'Do you tend to have violent outbursts, PG?'

'No, I don't think so ... I mean, I have my faults, God knows I make plenty of mistakes, but I'm not a violent man. Or I haven't been until now, not as far as I'm aware.'

'Is there anything to suggest that you did hurt the man in the picture?'

'What do you mean?'

'Bloodstains, for example. Or any injuries you might have sustained in a fight, ripped clothes.'

'No, no, nothing like that, but ... I mean, the picture, it's on my phone. My wife said I should go straight to the police. Maybe she's right, but I came here instead. I want to hire you and wait for you to finish your investigation before I decide what to do.'

Julia felt butterflies in her stomach, a moment of weightlessness. Her heart started pounding, and she looked down at the wristwatch that had once belonged to her father, saw the glare in the scratched glass and watched as the second hand began to slow.

Tick ... tick ... tick ...

The movement became more sluggish, eventually stopping entirely. The shadow of the second hand was like a grey thread across the face of the watch, pointing up towards the roman numeral nine.

Julia looked up at her prospective client, studying him through the particles of dust that were swirling through the air. The horizontal furrows on his forehead had deepened. His white hair was cut short, combed into a side parting, and she could make out a yellowed bruise beneath one eye, as though he had rubbed the skin a little too hard. His chin trembled softly as he pressed his lips together, trying to give an impression of composure.

'What are the alternatives?' she heard herself ask.

'My wife was so shocked when I showed her the picture ... She knows I wouldn't be able to live with myself if I found out I'd killed someone, I just couldn't.'

'No,' Julia whispered, taking note of the resigned tone in his voice.

'If you conclude it was me who hurt that man, then I'll take my punishment,' he said, looking down at his left wrist.

She followed his gaze and saw the two parallel tendons, the blue veins beneath his pale skin, and wondered whether he meant he would take his own life if he was guilty.

'Your punishment?' she repeated.

Her body grew heavy again, the second hand returning to its normal speed. PG tugged on his shirt sleeve and looked up at her.

'Yes, that's my plan . . . though I obviously don't want to take the fall for a crime I didn't commit. That's why I didn't go straight to the police. I'm from a rather well known family, you see – at least in Sundsvall and the forestry industry. We're old timber magnates, we own the Mannheim Group.'

'I've heard of that.'

'Yes, it . . .'

Julia opened her bag and pulled on a pair of thin leather gloves. She knew that PG would barely glance at the contract she was about to hand him. He would sign his name without a second's thought, and then he would want to shake her hand. He was a businessman, used to making quick decisions, and he couldn't bear to have this sword of Damocles hanging over him for a second longer than necessary.

'You came all the way from Sundsvall to engage my services,' she said slowly.

'I read about the case involving the china dolls.'

'I see.'

Two years ago, Julia had solved a case that garnered a lot of attention, and after that the well-paid, prestigious jobs started flooding in. It meant she could afford to pay herself a decent wage, and before long she also managed to leave her small apartment on the outskirts of the city, taking out a mortgage to buy the office and an adjoining apartment at this exclusive address in the heart of Stockholm.

'One last question, just to make sure I have all of the facts,' she said. 'Where was your phone last night?'

'I'd left it in the dining room. We had a big dinner for all the shareholders yesterday evening.'

'And you think someone else could have taken it?'

'That's what I'm hoping,' PG replied, a cautious note of optimism in his voice.

'Because you don't need to unlock a phone in order to take a picture,' she said.

PG nodded. 'That's what my wife tried to tell me.'

'Do you have any thoughts on the kind of investigation you'd like me to carry out?'

'Well, if this is a murder then I need to know who the killer is – even if it turns out to be me ... But other than that, I just need to know how and why this picture ended up on my phone.'

'I understand.'

'Obviously I'm hoping I'll be proved innocent, that this is all just a misunderstanding. And of course I hope the man in the picture isn't someone I know ... But either way, I need to know what's going on.'

'You want me to get to the truth,' Julia summarised, watching as his jaw tensed briefly.

She took a contract from the tray, slipped it into a plastic folder with the agency's logo on the front and set it down in front of him.

'This is my standard contract. I suggest you take it away and read it through, then get back in touch if you'd like me to start investigating.'

'I don't need to read it,' he said, taking out a pen, flicking through to the last page and signing his name. 'This can't wait. I'd really like you to come up to the family estate tomorrow, if at all possible. To Mannheim.'

'Tomorrow?'

'Yes, if you can,' he repeated.

'I'll try to make it work.'

'Everyone who was at the dinner will be there.'

'Then I'd like to start by speaking to each of them individually,' said Julia.

'Perfect.'

PG slipped his pen back into his breast pocket, got to his feet and held out his hand.

# 3

As soon as Per Günter Mott had left the office, Julia returned to her desk and took off her gloves. She felt a fluttering excitement in her chest. This was the perfect opportunity for her to take a first step closer to Sid.

She spent a moment or two trying to come up with a perfect opening line, but she quickly realised that doing so only made her nervous. Instead, she dug her phone out of her bag, hesitated for a moment, then scrolled slowly down her contacts list and pressed the tip of her index finger to his name.

'Sidney,' he answered.

'Hi. I'm sorry for calling while you're at work, but I ...'

Julia paused and swallowed, hard. She suddenly regretted making the call, wasn't ready to hear his voice in her ear.

'Julia? Has something happened?'

'No, there's just something I ... Thank you for the flowers, by the way.'

'I tried to call.'

'Did you?'

Her earring clinked against her phone. She could hear the rhythmic whirring of a photocopier in the background.

'I'll get straight to the point,' she said, heart racing. 'I know it's short notice, but I've just been hired on a job I'm going to struggle to manage on my own. I could really do with some help tomorrow, from someone with a driving licence and a knowledge of forensics, ideally a police officer ... And that made me think of you.'

'Hold on ...'

'I'll pay. It'll only take a few days.'

'Julia, I don't know—'

'I'll pay double,' she interrupted him.

'I just don't know if this is a good idea.'

'No, I agree, and I wouldn't ask if I didn't really need your help.'

'What's the case?'

Julia realised that her legs were shaking as she sat down and started to recap everything she knew about both the case and her new client.

'He's hired me to get to the bottom of what happened, which I like,' she rounded off.

In the brief pause on the other end of the line, Julia heard a light ticking sound. She imagined Sid standing at a poker table, dealing out cards. One by one, he swiped them from the deck and let them fall to the varnished surface, and then there was silence.

'I do actually have a few days' leave I could take,' he said.

'Is that a yes?'


Once they ended the call, her forced smile faltered and she broke down in tears. Julia pressed her hands to her face, waiting for it to pass. She rubbed her cheeks and leaned back against the chair, eventually managing to bring her breathing under control as she fantasised about changing the sign on the front door to *Mendelson & Stark Detective Agency*.

\* \* \*

Sidney Mendelson's right hand was relaxed on the wheel. The tyres roared against the tarmac as a fenced-off distribution plant raced by to the left of the car.

He had accepted her offer and said that he could pick her up after his shift, at two o'clock the next day, and now here they were, heading north together.

Julia found her eyes drifting down to his tanned fingers. He had a grubby-looking plaster on his thumb, and in another life she would have been able to scold him for that, help him to put on a new one. But those days were over.

Still, she had managed to convince him to tag along, and she would now do her very best to solve the case and show him just how good she was at her job in order to tempt him over to her side.

The best strategy for unearthing the truth was incredibly simple: you just had to listen carefully and deploy any questions strategically, the way a chess player moves their pieces. For Julia, that sometimes meant taking people by surprise with an unconventional directness. Other times, it meant holding off on asking the obvious questions in an attempt to appeal to a person's deeply human need to confess.

A combination of drugs and alcohol had left their new client with significant gaps in his memory from the day of the shareholders' meeting. He claimed he had started drinking at midday and that he had also taken fifty milligrams of hydroxyzine, a medication with a sedative, anti-anxiety effect lasting at least twelve hours.

PG Mott had explained that he had no idea how the image of a bound, bloody man had ended up on his phone. He wasn't sure whether he had taken the picture himself, but Julia could tell that he had his suspicions as to who the injured man might be. Either he couldn't bring himself to follow that thought through to its conclusion, or he simply refused to share his thoughts because there was no way he could know for sure – the mystery man had a bag over his head, after all.

If all this was correct, then the reason he had given for coming to Julia was likely also true: that he wanted her to get to the bottom of what happened. It wasn't an attempt to evade justice. PG Mott simply couldn't stand the thought that he might have been the one to injure the man. The whole situation was unbearable to him.

Julia had explained that the only exceptions to the agency's duty of confidentiality involved terrorism and offences involving children, but PG had refused to forward the image on his phone. It was as though he just couldn't accept that it really existed, as though he was longing for the moment when he could finally delete it, but also knew it would stubbornly hang over him until he had been cleared of all suspicion.

Julia would likely have to insist that he shared it with her, but she hadn't wanted to scare him off by pushing him too soon.

They drove out onto the motorway bridge over the Dala River, the water down below as smooth as a sheet on a washing line.

Bright sunlight filled the car, and Julia closed her eyes.

She felt a thud as they crossed the far end of the bridge.

Through her eyelids, she saw the shadows of pylons racing by, and then everything went dark. She realised that they must be driving through another tunnel of deep green forest, and she opened her eyes again.

'I took seven days' leave in the end,' said Sid.

'Do you really think I need seven days to solve a case?'

'Julia ... Unless you've undergone some sort of personality transplant, you do sometimes have a tendency to come to hasty conclusions, and don't tell me—'

'It's all part of the strategy.'

'And don't tell me it's all part of the strategy,' he rounded off with a smirk.

'Maybe not always.'

'I just wanted to remind you of that.'

'OK.'

'I don't mean anything by it.'

'No, I know. I appreciate you warning me ... about myself.'

'You're not listening.'

'I am.'

'No.'

'I'll listen if you say you want to take me to dinner,' she said, though she knew it would make him uncomfortable.

Logging roads and clearings raced by behind tall wildlife fences, and they drove on in silence.

After a while, Sid started talking about needing to fill the tank before they got to Hudiksvall.

'Sorry,' she whispered.

'What?'

Julia hated the fact that her leg prevented her from driving, but the knowledge that her hand was resting on a bottle of water in the cup holder just a few inches away from Sid's thigh gave her butterflies.

'It feels strange,' she said. 'To be in a car, with you . . . I was about to say as though everything was back to normal.'

'The years pass, and you end up getting used to . . . to the new normal,' he replied.

'But are you happy?'

'Could we change the subject? I agreed to tag along because you needed help with the case. Can we just stick to that?'

Julia knew she was paying him far too much, but she also knew that his police officer's eye and his knowledge of forensics would come in useful. Besides, he was the only person who had a calming influence on her when she got carried away. There was an impatience in Julia that occasionally led her to skip over logical assumptions and draw hasty conclusions – though they did often prove to be correct in the end.

She really could have done with him by her side on her last day as a clerk, when she could no longer bear to just sit passively, listening to the case. Instead, she had got to her feet, pointed at the accused and called him a pathetic fucking wife beater.

'I checked with the local force and all the hospitals around Sundsvall, from Gävle up to Umeå,' he said.

'No one who could be our man from the picture?' she asked, though his tone of voice had already told her the answer.

'The closest was a young man in the morgue in Gävle. Road traffic accident. Driving his motorcycle without a helmet. But—'

'The man in the picture isn't young.'

'No,' he whispered.

'What are you thinking?'

'Obviously I haven't seen the picture yet, but from your description it sounds like a head injury.'

'The sack was bloody around where his temple should have been, all the way down to his throat,' she confirmed.

'Right, and if you take the capillary action into consideration – the way the material wicks the blood upwards – that would suggest the injury was roughly here,' said Sid, pointing to his own face at the same level as his ear.

'Anything else?'

'Just that we can probably also assume he was dead when the picture was taken,' Sidney replied. 'I mean, from what you've said there was a lot of blood ... He'd go into a state of shock almost immediately, and that would make his breathing rapid. But you didn't mention any stains in front of his mouth.'

'There weren't any.'

Sid was right, thought Julia. If the man hadn't died immediately then he had likely gone into circulatory failure. Losing that much blood results in a sharp drop in blood pressure, which means insufficient oxygenation. The body tries to compensate with a quick pulse and rapid breathing. It was a bit like a whirlpool, dragging the dying person to the middle of the maelstrom and then down to the bottom.

'You're right,' she said. 'He's dead. I agree.'

'Is this where I shout hallelujah?' he asked drily.

'I always agree with you.'

'Sure,' he replied, trying to hold back a smile.

'OK, I know ... But you wouldn't be here if you didn't know you were right,' she said. 'If you thought there was even the slightest chance of saving the man in the picture you would have tried to get me to talk the client into handing himself in.'

They passed the industrial area on the northern outskirts of Gävle and then continued through large areas of cleared forest. Evening light flooded into the car from the west, and they both put on their sunglasses.

'A dead man who doesn't match the description of anyone reported missing in the area,' said Julia.

'Not everyone who disappears is missing,' he countered.

Julia turned her head and studied him. She wasn't sure whether Sidney's time as a detective had changed his appearance or whether her sense of what a police officer should look like had been shaped by him. His hair was cropped like a Roman soldier's, his nose straight and his eyes a shade of chestnut brown. He was also big and muscular, with a fairly deep voice.

'I can't exactly claim I'm happy,' Sid said without warning, answering her earlier question. 'I mean ... that has nothing to do with us, that's just how it is.'

'Maybe.'

'What about you? How are you ... these days?' he asked without taking his eyes off the road.

'Good,' she replied.

'I hear you're on Tinder?'

'Aren't you?'

'Nope.'

'A friend made me sign up,' she hurried to explain. 'But honestly, I just feel like the butt of a bad joke on there.'

'You should give it a chance.'

'I don't have time.'

'Just check to see who's interested,' he said.

'Stop.'

'Haven't you done that?'

'I opened the app once, but it wasn't for me. I can't handle that sort of thing,' she said.

'Love or people?'

A buzzard circled the landscape of tree stumps and deep machine tracks.

'It's easier for you,' she said.

Julia saw the corner of his mouth curl upwards slightly, though she knew he didn't like this game.

'I'm not sure about that, but yeah, there's a colleague I've started having lunch with,' he said, blushing slightly.

'Of course there is.'

'She's in surveillance.'

'Jewish?'

'What difference does that make?' His breathing grew heavier, his jaw tensing.

'Have you finally found yourself a nice Jewish girl?' Julia teased. 'Your mum can be happy at last.'

'Mum was happy about you.'

The logging area gave way to more dark pines, and Sidney's face was cast into shadow yet again.

Julia had a sudden vision of him on their wedding day, in the soft light beneath the chuppah. She remembered circling him seven times. He had been grinning at first, but he grew serious as she completed the circuits, symbolically binding them together.

Fragments of the past swept by: the Sheva Brachot, the taste of wine, the way Sidney broke the glass beneath his foot without taking his eyes off her.

Julia realised what she was doing and dragged herself back to the present, taking her notepad out of her bag.

'Per Günter, or PG as he likes to be called, is the managing director of the family company, with a thirty-five per cent share. He's fifty-six, and he lives in the manor house, Mannheim, with his wife,' she said.

'So they're rich?'

'They own a lot of forest, and the manor house is supposed to be fantastic, but the whole thing is actually a little opaque ... It's set up as a group, with the forestry business tied to one company, the majority of capital and assets to another. There are five different holding companies, which means a whole bunch of accounts, partial tax years, dividends and contributions.'

'I'd be happy to take a look,' said Sid.

'Per Günter and his brother Werther are fourth-generation timber magnates,' she continued. 'Their father Sylvester took over the manor after his father, Leopold, who took over after his father, Mannheim Mott, who started and built one of the biggest forestry empires in Europe in the late nineteenth century.'

Julia thought through everything she had asked PG during their meeting. She was increasingly convinced he had been telling the truth when he said he didn't remember a thing. His fears had seemed genuine, but there was also something unsettling about him. For some strange reason, he reminded her of a waterlogged field where the crops had begun to wither and rot.

The likely murder of the unidentified man had taken place on the same day as the annual shareholders' meeting, when all family members with a stake in the company were gathered at Mannheim. PG had left his mobile phone in the dining room, and when he woke the next morning the image of the dead man had been in his camera reel. Rather than follow his wife's advice and go to the police, he had jumped straight into his car and driven to Stockholm to engage Julia's services.

Sid turned off at a petrol station just before Söderhamn.

Julia put on her leather gloves and got out of the car as he filled the tank, heading into the shop to buy sandwiches and coffee. She used her stick to open the door, heard the bell ring, and headed for the coffee machine.

A man in leather trousers and a blue silk shirt was blowing on a cup of coffee over by the counter. He had a ponytail and a moustache with waxed tips, and he was chatting to the shop assistant. He had just paid for a scratch card, and Julia heard him saying that he had bought his daughter a blow-up flamingo for her seventh birthday.

'But it'd be nice to have a pool to put it in, you know?' he said as he took the scratch card.

Julia hesitated in the aisle between the sweets and biscuits, debating whether or not to turn and leave. The shelves towered above her, and the claustrophobic feeling of being trapped made her heart race.

The man with the ponytail moved along the counter, studying the various hotdogs glistening on the rollers inside.

Julia took a deep breath and walked over to the coffee machine. She put her cane down on the bench, grabbed two large paper cups and filled them with strong black coffee before pushing the plastic lids on top.

The machine whirred as it ground more beans.

Julia carried the two cups over to the glass counter, reached for her cane and then turned to the refrigerator to pick a couple of sandwiches.

Ciabatta Caesar, Club Sandwich, Tomato and Mozzarella.

She had just reached out to open the door when she felt something brush against the back of her neck. The panicked feeling of being tossed onto a pile of cold body parts surged through her, and she staggered to the side and knocked over a stand of wiper blades. Before she had time to think, she had wheeled around and lashed out with her cane, striking the man hard on the cheek.

'What the fuck! I was just straightening your collar,' he groaned.

'Sorry, I didn't mean ...'

'Jesus Christ.'

He clutched his red cheek, backing away from her in confusion.

With shaking hands, Julia tried to pick up the stand of wiper blades. The shop assistant came running over, and Julia heard the bell above the door ring as the man left.

'What happened?' the assistant asked.

'I have to go,' Julia blurted out as she snatched up the long, slim wrappers from the floor.

'Just leave them.'

'Sorry.'

'Did he touch you? Did he?' the shop assistant asked. 'Do you want to report him?'

'No, I—'

'I've got his card details in the system, the whole thing is on CCTV.'

'I can't, I have to go.'

'OK ... But at least take the coffee, it's on me.'

Julia hurried out of the shop, got back into the car and fastened her seat belt. Her hands were still trembling far too much for her to be able to drink her coffee.

'What just happened, Julia? You're shaking,' said Sidney.

'There was a man in there ... He touched the back of my neck.'

'You need to be careful.'

'I know, I just got a shock.'

'Close your eyes and focus on your breathing,' he said, starting the engine.

# 4

The forests of Hälsingland had closed in on the car yet again, and the road in front of them seemed to stretch straight up into the sky, heading due north forever.

Julia focused on the monotonous droning of the tyres against the tarmac and felt her heart rate slowly drop.

'Feeling better?' Sid asked.

'Yes, it's just ... I'm so sick of being this way. It's embarrassing, I don't know what to do ... I don't even recognise myself when that sort of thing happens.'

Her post-traumatic stress disorder made physical touch incredibly complex, particularly any unexpected skin-on-skin contact. She had spent years attending the Trauma Centre, devoting hundreds of hours to conversational therapy and CBT, yet she still couldn't touch upon her loss without having a panic attack. Lately, however, she and her therapist had made some progress in approaching her grief by talking about an imaginary photograph of the funeral.

In order to avoid coming too close to the bottomless pit of anxiety, Julia imagined that the picture had been taken from high above, looking straight down into the church. Through this made-up photograph, she had been able to describe a young girl who had lowered her crutches to the stone floor. She sat alone at the front of the church, surrounded by the intoxicating scent of thousands of flowers, eyes fixed on the four coffins in front of her.

Julia had been prescribed countless medications over the years, tried alternative therapies and regularly practised yoga, but so far she had only found two things that brought her any real sense of calm.

One was helping other people navigate their way through crisis. As she worked to find the truth, she could forget everything else and focus on their faces, their words.

The other was her life with Sid, his love and patience. But that was gone for good now, the pieces scattered among the rest of the smoking wreckage on the side of a mountain.

'Your mum never liked that you were the one who did all our washing ... bloodstains and make-up on the towels,' said Julia.

'I like washing.'

'I liked watching you hang my knickers and bras out to dry.'

'What?' he asked, smirking. 'What about it?'

'Nothing.' She laughed.

The forest opened out onto a landscape of fields and red wooden barns. They passed a small hamlet called Sodom and exchanged a silent glance.

'All mysteries and secrets that ever existed are connected,' Sid said after a while.

'Do you think so?'

'According to the Hekhalot texts,' he clarified.

Sidney's mother was Jewish, his father a Marxist, and he had grown up to be thoroughly secular – though he accepted certain rituals for his mother's sake, and liked to amuse himself by quoting Jewish mystics.


They left the E4 just north of Sundsvall and spent the next twenty-two kilometres driving through dense green forest.

It was much later than expected by the time they reached the edge of the estate. Beneath a florid cast-iron archway with the name Mannheim emblazoned in gold, the gates were open.

'I'm really glad you're here,' said Julia, her voice barely audible.

They turned off and followed the road through yet more forest, catching flashes of a small river glittering between the trunks. Solitary wooden houses and shacks raced by, and the landscape opened out onto meadows and fields once again.

'Not long until we get an idea of how this investigation is going to pan out,' said Julia. 'Sometimes it's like going from one interrogation room to another, but the best thing is always just to spend time together, as though we're all old friends ...'

'You're trying to tell me something, aren't you?'

'Yes; that we should just chat to them like normal, but whenever we get to a more critical moment, it's best you let me take over.'

'Well, you are Julia Stark,' he said with a smile.

'You can talk, it's not that – we need to work together to keep the conversation going, in a friendly way ... Just remember that it's important to wait until you've made eye contact before you ask any key questions.'

'Got it,' said Sid.

'And it's probably best if you keep quiet about being a police officer, too.'

He shot her a quick look. 'Why?'

'Some people don't exactly find it relaxing to be around the police ...'

'No?'

'Per Günter might have a record,' she said.

'True.'

'Can you find out?'

'I *can*, but it would be unethical.'

'Seriously?' she asked wearily.

'Only certain employers – within health and social care, for example – can request a person's record.'

'You're sick in the head, you know that? Surely you can just check—'

'I work in the public sector. You're a private operator,' he cut her off. 'If it turns out you only asked me to tag along so you could get access to the police databases, I'll put a stop to this right now.'

'You know we were married for seven years, don't you?'

'I do.'

'Because you're being super formal right now.'

'It's good for you to have boundaries.'

'What?'

'It's good for you to have boundaries.'

'What?'

On the banks of a small, dark lake that had formed above the dam on the river, there was a small brick building with a jetty surrounded by bulrushes and reeds.

The sun had begun to dip behind the forest, making the crowns of the trees look like they were ablaze.

The road took them down an avenue to a grand manor house. It had a sloping black roof and a glazed brick facade with row upon row of French windows. The gravel driveway was meticulously raked, ending in a turning circle around a neat lawn with a sundial on a granite block.

As Sidney switched off the engine, the door opened and PG came out onto the steps with a red-haired woman in trousers and a thin cardigan.

Julia grabbed her cane and struggled out of the car. Straightening up, she realised just how stiff she was after the long drive. The evening air was warm and smelled like pine and moss. The birds were chirping, and the setting sun glittered in the half-moon window on the top floor.

Sidney took their bags from the boot and, out of habit, reached out and supported Julia's arm. Her body remembered his touch, and it seemed to echo through her. Resonating in her heart like a broken violin string as they made their way towards the building.

'Welcome to Mannheim,' said the woman. 'I'm Monika, the gold-digger of the family.'

'We've been married thirty years,' PG hastened to add.

'But that's what my husband thought of me when we first met – which is actually rather flattering, looking back now,' she said with a laugh.

'I'd like you to know that Monika takes this just as seriously as I do.'

'Yes, yes. Apologies if I've given the wrong impression – I think that might be my superpower.'

Sidney let go of the suitcase and shook hands with the Motts while Julia propped herself up on her cane, pretending to be reading a message on her phone until the moment had passed.

'Please, come in,' said PG.

They followed him up the steps and into an enormous entrance hall with a cobweb-strewn chandelier, wall sconces and a grand staircase.

'What a house,' Sid gushed.

'Designed by Fritz Eckert,' PG explained. 'Who was also responsible for Antuna Manor, the Royal Stables, the Curmanska Villa ...'

A woman in a simple black dress and a white apron said a subdued hello and took their coats. She looked to be in her sixties, with nervy blue eyes and dark hair gathered in a tight bun at the nape of her neck.

'Amelie here will show you to your rooms,' said Monika, pausing with a frown. 'Or perhaps I have the wrong end of the stick ... You did want separate rooms, didn't you?'

'Yes, we're just colleagues,' Sid reassured her.

Julia smiled and nodded, but a wave of longing washed over her.

'A real-life Sherlock and Watson,' Monika mumbled.

'Something like that,' said Sid.

PG was chewing on a ragged nail, but he stopped what he was doing and gave himself a smack on the hand when he noticed Julia's eyes on him.

'You'd be making my job a lot easier if you would share the picture of the man with me,' she said.

'I'd really rather not. I'd prefer—'

'It's imperative.'

'Of course, of course. Sorry,' he said with a nod, handing his phone to his wife.

'Luddite,' Monika teased.

A moment later, Julia's phone pinged with a message.

'Thank you.'

'There's one thing I'd like to ask you right away,' said Monika, keeping her voice low. 'It's not illegal, is it? To have a picture like that on his phone?'

'No,' said Sidney.

'Because imagine if someone just sent you a weird picture like that. What are you supposed to do then?'

'But this picture wasn't sent to PG's phone,' Julia pointed out.

'Dinner,' PG mumbled, changing the subject.

'Yes, of course, that reminds me. We thought it might be nice to eat dinner together this evening, at eight o'clock. What do you think?' said Monika, though she immediately seemed to doubt herself. 'Sorry, it's just we have no idea how these things work. Maybe you'd rather eat on your own so that you can get to work . . . ? Though it is getting late.'

'We'd be happy to eat dinner with you,' said Julia.

'See?' said PG, nodding to his wife.

'As I said yesterday, I'd very much like to speak to everyone who was here on Sunday,' said Julia.

'Don't worry about tomorrow, because tomorrow will worry about itself, as they say in the Bible,' said Monika. 'PG has planned both a grand tour and meetings with everyone.'

'Yes, it's all arranged,' said PG. 'You'll meet the rest of our little family tomorrow.'

'Lucky you,' Monika sighed.

PG took them through his plans for the next day, and then the woman called Amelie led Julia and Sidney up the creaking stairs, down a long corridor, to their rooms.

'Thanks,' Sidney told her, putting their bags down.

'Your hosts will be waiting in the drawing room on the ground floor at eight.'

'Wonderful,' Julia said with a smile.

Amelie made her way back towards the stairs, leaving them alone. Sid shot Julia an amused look, pausing for a moment before he spoke.

'So, have you solved the mystery yet?'

'Which one?'

'You'll be a Kabbalist before long.'

'I'll take this room,' said Julia.

She used her cane to open the door closest to her, wheeling her suitcase inside and across a yellow oriental rug.

The window was open to let in the breeze, but the scent of pine soap, wood and old fabric was still lingering in the air.

There were signs of water damage on the ornate silk wallpaper, Julia noticed. A freestanding wardrobe made from dark, almost black wood had been pushed up against one wall, beside a florid walnut desk and a canopy bed.

Julia opened her suitcase in the middle of the floor, unpacked her underwear and toiletry bag and hung her dresses on the padded hangers in the wardrobe.

PG had written to her yesterday evening to say that while she and Sid were free to dress however they liked, he thought he should mention that his family had a penchant for tradition, and that his wife had suggested Julia might like to bring a couple of cocktail dresses, an evening gown and possibly also a pair of trousers and a blazer to wear in the woods.

Julia closed the wardrobe doors and moved over to the window to shut it. The glass was old and warped, which made the forest outside ripple as her eyes scanned the landscape.

She sat down in the chair, took out her phone and spent a moment studying the image of the dead man before forwarding it to Sid.

What possible motive could PG have for driving all the way down to Stockholm to show her the photograph of the body if he was in fact guilty of murdering the man – and conscious of having done so, at that?

Logic suggested that the gaps in his memory must be real, assuming this wasn't simply an attempt at some sort of reverse-reverse psychology.

# 5

PG AND MONIKA WERE WAITING for their guests in the old study just off from the large drawing room on the ground floor. The tall leaded windows looked out onto the forest, and the floor was hidden beneath a tobacco-coloured Persian carpet. Behind a mahogany and copper bar counter, countless bottles of spirits glittered on the floor-to-ceiling shelves.

PG was now wearing a dark suit, and he seemed to have applied a little blusher to his cheeks. Monika had also changed, into a classic grey Chanel dress. Her dyed red hair was slicked back, and she was wearing a three-strand necklace of yellowed pearls around her neck.

'Ah, the youngsters are here,' said PG.

'He calls you the youngsters because you're both so beautiful,' Monika explained.

'Respectfully and jealously,' PG said with a smile.

A painting of a naked woman wading out into a bay hung on one of the walls, her plump white bottom shining bright in the dappled light.

'Is that an Anders Zorn?' asked Julia.

'Yes, he was a frequent guest here some years ago,' PG told her, adopting an anecdotal tone. 'According to my grandfather, he was on the verge of losing a game of strip poker and bought his way out with this ...'

'Saving his own bare backside from public view,' said Monika.

'Something like that.'

'Well, I think it's time for an aperitif, don't you? That way perhaps you'll get the chance to witness one of my husband's blackouts for yourselves,' said Monika, gesturing towards the bottles.

'She doesn't mean to joke about—'

'Oh, come on,' she laughed, making her way over to the bar.

'I mix a mean drink,' said PG, turning to Julia. 'Can I interest you in a vodka martini, a dry martini, a cosmopolitan or a Cuba libre?'

'I'll take a vodka with ice,' she replied.

'Sounds complicated,' PG laughed, turning to Sidney.

'A Cuba libre. Why not?'

'Perfect,' said PG, moving behind the bar.

He shook vodka and ice, strained the liquid into a martini glass and then used a pair of tongs to add a large ice cube.

'My husband thinks I talk too much when I'm nervous,' said Monika.

'No,' PG protested. 'What I said—'

'Just wait, please ... And because I do – he's right about that, as I'm sure you've already noticed – I want to be clear that all of this makes me incredibly anxious.'

'Of course,' said Sid, taking the glass PG held out and handing it to Julia.

'Thank you,' she said.

'When PG showed me that ghastly photograph on his phone, I got such a shock, I really did,' Monika continued. 'I was so upset, I raised my voice, tried to get him to remember, to swear he was innocent.'

'But he couldn't do that,' Julia said quietly.

'That's why I came to you... We need to know,' PG explained. 'The whole thing is absurd: waking up one morning and not knowing whether or not you murdered a man the night before.'

He speared an olive on a cocktail stick and passed another glass to his wife.

'Memory loss of this kind is very rarely total. There are often islands of memory amid the fog,' Julia pointed out.

'I have no idea, perhaps you're right. But mine aren't caused by any neurological issues, embarrassingly enough. They're simply the result of too much to drink in too short a space of time.'

He took down a bottle of rum from the shelf behind him and began to mix two Cuba libres.

'He's not an alcoholic,' said Monika. 'I know that's probably how it sounds, but... but these things happen so infrequently.'

'Is there a pattern?' asked Julia.

'No,' replied PG. 'Or rather, I'm sure there is, but I have no idea what triggers any of this ... It's as though I just *have* to drink, and when I come round I can no longer remember why.'

'Or what you said or did,' Monika added.

'But you think you could have injured the man in the photograph?' asked Sid.

'No, I don't, actually ... If I did, I'm not sure I would have been brave enough to come to you.'

'Well, cheers to that,' Monika muttered.

PG came out from behind the bar with two highball glasses, and Sid nodded in thanks as he took one of them.

'Cheers,' said PG.

Julia took a sip of her drink and then lowered the glass to the scratched counter. Her fingers had left small, clear ovals in the condensation. The sharp vodka burned her tongue.

'Very nice,' said Sid, looking down at his rum and coke.

'I'd like to know whether you recognised the man in the photograph,' said Julia, turning to Monika.

'No, I ... Should I?'

'It's just a question,' Julia explained. 'You can see quite a lot of his body. His clothes, the background.'

'Couldn't it just be some homeless person who fell and hurt himself?' Monika asked. 'I don't mean to belittle anything, but—'

'His hands are bound,' said Sid.

'Are they? Gosh, maybe I didn't look closely enough ... Forgive me, I just saw all that blood and panicked.'

They sipped their drinks in silence as the trees grew darker against the pale sky on the other side of the large windows. It was as though the looming presence of the forest was surrounding them on all sides, growing denser and more impenetrable.

Monika met Julia's eye.

'It gets rather dark out here,' she said, as though she had read her mind. 'For someone used to living by the coast, it can be a little jarring, but I've grown to love it. It feels so safe, almost like we're protected by all the tall pines. I'll never forget when PG brought me out here for the first time, I felt like a princess in a fairy tale.'

'I was born in these forests, and I plan to die here too,' PG announced somewhat pompously.

'And you?' asked Sid, turning to Monika.

'My parents ran a small hotel on the outskirts of Stockholm. I don't feel any need to die in a forest,' she said with a laugh, dabbing something from the corner of her mouth. 'I'd rather not die at all, to be perfectly honest.'

'But she does share my love of our land,' said PG.

'That's true,' Monika replied, cocking her head.

'She's the perfect wife for an old school forest owner,' he continued. He sounded slightly robotic, suggesting he had said the same thing countless times before.

'I'm actually part of the aristocracy ... A wonderful branch without any assets, I might add. I hate the House of the Nobility, I hate the privileges, the misogynist structure; it's absurd that something like that still exists in this day and age,' said Monika, pretending to shoot herself in the head.

'See what I mean?' PG said with a smile, raising his glass in a toast.

Julia did the same. It was clear to her that PG was trying to be cordial, acting like he was simply hosting a dinner party for a group of old friends, but his eyes were also heavy from a lack of sleep, deep lines carved around his mouth.

She noticed that Monika seemed relieved when Amelie opened the door and announced that dinner was ready.

They were ushered into a grand dining room with an enormous crystal chandelier on the ceiling. The walls were clad with dark panels inset with tapestries depicting various hunting scenes.

Around the huge dining table, there were eighteen chairs with chipped, dented armrests. Candles flickered in the silver candelabra in the middle of the white tablecloth, and one end of the room was almost entirely dominated by a large green marble fireplace. The windows looked out onto the lake they had seen when they arrived earlier. The pale sky was reflected in the still water, shimmering like silver in the darkness outside.

'Where exactly was your phone?' asked Sid.

'Right here, on the dresser,' replied PG.

He led them over to the narrow service corridor between the kitchen and the dining room and patted a shelf on the inbuilt cabinet housing the linens and silverware.

'Shall we take our seats?' Monika asked.

# 6

Amelie had set four places at one end of the enormous dining table, each with a starched white napkin and china monogrammed with *S. M.* in florid gold lettering. They left their glasses on the serving trolley, and Monika told each of them where to sit.

'S. M. stands for Sylvester Mott,' PG explained. 'He was my father and—'

'Quite the character,' Monika filled in, a note of sarcasm in her voice.

'My father commanded respect,' said PG.

'He was an awful, terrifying man. I'll tell you that because PG won't . . . At least until his illness. That blunted the edges a little.'

'I'm trying to honour his memory.'

'As am I,' she said, looking her husband straight in the eye.

PG opened his mouth to speak, but he seemed to change his mind as Amelie came in with the serving trolley and a bottle of red wine.

Their first course consisted of a small piece of grilled veal on a bed of rocket, with crushed black pepper, grated Parmesan and a squeeze of lemon.

As they ate, Julia stole glances at her ex-husband. With the light behind him, the downy hair on his face seemed to glow. Her eyes drifted down to his tanned hand. He no longer wore his wedding ring, and the pale band it had once left on his finger was long gone – as was hers. Julia watched him chatting, saw his mouth moving, but she didn't hear a single word he said. She was falling through time again, into the sparse intervals, a memory opening up: they were in bed, dipping slices of apple into honey and drinking strong wine that his mother had brought back from Tel Aviv.

Julia swallowed hard, forcing herself back to the present.

'So you left your phone on the dresser in the service corridor the evening of the shareholders' meeting, and it was still there the next morning?' she asked, looking up at PG.

'Yes,' he replied.

'What time that morning?'

'Before seven. I've got an inbuilt alarm clock,' PG explained, jabbing his forehead. 'I always wake up at six. It's like my body thinks I still have to go out and work in the forest.'

'And who else was here on Sunday?' Julia asked. 'You and Monika …'

'My second cousins. Björn, André and Siri.'

'And Amelie, I assume?'

'Yes, of course.'

'No one else?'

'Not as far as we know, no.'

'Monika?'

'No, just the usual dream team,' she replied.

'Any deliveries? Tradespeople?'

'No.'

'Other employees? Forestry workers, additional serving staff ... ? Gardeners?'

'Just Amelie.'

'Tell me about your second cousins,' said Julia, lowering her cutlery to the plate.

'They each have a ten per cent stake in the company, and they live in the houses on the banks of the river, upstream of here,' PG told her. 'There's a clause in my grandfather's will that says we have to meet twice a week, at least one representative from each branch of the family ...'

'It's claustrophobic,' Monika spoke up with a faux shudder.

'Yes, it can be. But money has been set aside for this, and our dinners have been getting increasingly lavish – possibly so that we can actually stand the sight of one another.'

'I don't know whether the idea was to turn us into a bunch of drunks, but if it was then the old man's project has been quite the success,' said Monika.

'We're all stuck here at Mannheim, as though we're in some sort of Sartre play,' said PG. 'My older brother Werther is the only one who has managed to escape.'

'It's like a sect,' Monika agreed with a laugh.

PG got up and fetched a framed photograph from a small table by the wall, setting it down in front of Julia.

'Despite the age difference, we all used to play together,' he said. 'Little Siri is only three here, and Werther must have been ... eighteen, I think.'

It was a black and white photograph, taken in front of a row of tall sunflowers. The five heirs were standing in descending height order, like the pipes in an organ. Julia studied it closely. The eldest boy, Werther, was staring straight at the camera with his chin held high and a slight smile on his face. PG was next, with dirty knees and a plaster on the bridge of his nose. The remaining three children were all considerably shorter. The two boys were standing with their arms around each other's shoulders, and the young girl was laughing at them.

'So their dad was your father's cousin?' asked Sid.

'Exactly,' replied PG. 'Augustus Mott. My father gave him a thirty per cent stake in the company, which they now share between them.'

'A stroke of genius,' Monika muttered.

They thanked Amelie for their starters as she cleared the plates away, and there was no time to resume their conversation before she was back with the next course. Without a word, the older woman served fried turbot with rice timbales and seafood sauce on a puff pastry base, accompanied by a bottle of Rhône wine.

'You were telling us about your second cousins,' Sid reminded PG once Amelie had left the room.

'There isn't much else to say.'

'Not if you're trying to avoid the truth,' said Monika.

PG cleared his throat.

'The eldest of the three, Björn, is a passionate craftsman, incredibly skilled at renovating antique furniture. He's the one who restored the chandelier,' he said, gesturing towards the study.

'PG's father took a gun to it while he was drunk, apparently,' Monika added with a satisfied smile. 'What was left of it hung like some sort of bad conscience in the Brewhouse for years – until Björn managed to get hold of the exact Bohemian crystal needed to fix it.'

'You have to see it. It's a real masterpiece.'

'I said earlier that PG isn't an alcoholic,' Monika went on. 'But that might be more in comparison to Björn than anything. The man's been practically legless for the past five years.'

'Monika ...' PG rebuked her, a smile playing on his lips.

'Sorry, but from that perspective not much has changed ... He still just sits around, drinking and getting angry, falling asleep with his mouth wide open.'

'It's fair to say he has his problems, but his younger brother André looks after him. It's a miracle he has the patience,' said PG.

'They run a business together. They're dependent on each other,' said Monika.

'And the third of your cousins?' asked Sid, pointing to the young girl in the photograph.

'Yes, Siri ... What is there to say about her?' Monika drummed her fingers on the table. 'She's not polyamorous, she's ... What do you say, PG? I'd never use the word whore, but ...'

'That was uncalled for,' said PG.

Monika turned to Julia and Sid, an impassive look on her face.

'Sorry, perhaps I should try to hide the fact that Siri is rather an awful person ...'

'I feel sorry for her,' PG spoke up.

'Of course. I'm sure it's all my fault.' Monika smiled.

'No, I—'

'You know that it was me – not her – who tried to straighten everything out before the meeting. I knew I wouldn't be able to stand yet another uncomfortable dinner full of taunts,' Monika explained to PG, keeping her voice low.

'I know ...'

'Monika sipped her wine, dabbed her mouth with a napkin and then turned to Sid and Julia with a troubled smile.

'She and I got into the rowing boat and went out on the lake. I took coffee and buns, thought it could be a chance for us to work through our problems and be honest with each other,' she explained. 'And it was all going so well until we got to certain subjects ... Well, she started screaming at me and calling me a witch as I rowed back to shore ...'

'At least it was an honest attempt,' PG mumbled.

Silence settled over the room, and Julia cut off a piece of turbot, coated it in sauce and raised her fork to her mouth.

'This is delicious,' she said quietly.

Sid's plate was already empty, his cutlery neatly stacked on top. Julia had often complained that he used to wolf down his food while they were married, but she was happy to see that he still had his appetite.

'You said that Björn, André and Siri each own ten per cent of the company?' asked Sid.

'Yes. We have a thirty-five per cent stake, and so does Werther,' said PG.

'And Werther is your older brother?'

'Yes, but he wasn't at the meeting.'

'Why not?' asked Sid.

'It's been years since he last came,' PG replied evasively.

'We've missed his warmth and enthusiasm, the way he brings the group together,' said Monika.

'She's being sarcastic,' PG hurriedly explained.

'I remember the last time he was here, when he tried to help you fix your suit,' Monika said ambiguously.

PG seemed uncomfortable, and he raised a hand to his wrinkled neck, as though to excuse her thoughtlessness.

'In all honesty, my brother is really quite like our father ...'

'He's a psychopath,' Monika muttered.

'Werner is a recluse,' PG explained. 'He keeps himself to himself, spends most of his time in his hunting lodge over in Jämtland. He usually appoints me as his proxy before every AGM, because he knows we think alike. But he didn't do that this time, and I was so stressed out by the thought that he might turn up that, like I said, I took a couple of Atarax at lunch, just to be able to cope.'

# 7

Julia and Monika strolled after the two men when they left the dining room, moving through to the drawing room with the grand piano. PG said something to Sid, who laughed and thumped him on the back.

As they made their way into the study where the enormous crystal chandelier hung from the ceiling, Sid turned around and met Julia's eye. He smiled.

'Just colleagues, hmm?' Monika teased.

'These days, yes,' she replied, with much more longing in her voice than she had intended.

They came out into a square library with a worn parquet floor.

'We call this the Red Room,' PG announced in a gruff voice.

The fraying velvet curtains were open, and the colourful stained glass windows looked out onto the garden.

Two of the walls were entirely hidden behind floor-to-ceiling bookshelves, complete with ladders. On the fourth wall, there were four magnificent oil portraits of each generation's first-born son, in chronological order. Mannheim, Leopold, Sylvester and Werther.

'Why the Red Room?' asked Julia.

'There's always been a red rug in here. Invaluable thing. Legend has it that my grandfather bought it in exchange for a box of Cuban cigars in Kerman,' said PG, moving straight over to the bar cart, where the carafes and bottles of whisky, cognac, grappa, port and various liqueurs glittered in the soft light.

'So where is it now?' Julia asked.

'At the dry cleaner,' PG replied, offering no further explanation.

Monika set out four hardwood coasters on the low table and gestured to the brown leather armchairs. Julia and Sid both took a seat, then Monika did the same. PG asked what the youngsters would like to drink and then got to work preparing them.

In order to avoid any physical contact, Julia picked up a thick book on Swedish forestry just as he arrived with her grappa.

'Thank you,' she said as he put it down on the coaster.

'Shall I try to summarise everything we know so far?' asked Sid.

'Good idea,' said PG, handing him a glass of malt whisky before taking a seat in the fourth armchair.

'Following the shareholders' meeting and dinner the day before yesterday, PG left his phone on the dresser in the service corridor. At 23.25, the same phone was used to take a photograph of a man – bound, bloody and likely dead, with a bag over his head. At around seven the next morning, the phone was back where PG had left it the night before. Assuming there was no one else in the house, there are only six people who could have taken the photograph.'

'Of which I'm the most likely,' said PG, taking a large swig of whisky.

'Not necessarily,' said Julia.

'The problem is that I have absolutely no memory of what happened that evening.'

'So how do we move forward?' asked Monika, studying Sid with a blank face.

'We'll start by finding out which of the six had the means to take the picture just before half eleven,' he replied.

'Well, you can rule me out,' said Monika. 'A bottle of port had been knocked over in here and Amelie and I were trying to save the rug.'

'Even though it was almost midnight?' asked Sid.

'That's the hard part about managing an inheritance,' she replied. 'The fear of ruining something that's meant to be celebrated for generations to come.'

'It was all my fault, apparently,' said PG, stifling a burp.

'His movements get a little over the top sometimes – flamboyant, you might say. It's actually rather charming, to a degree ... The port was all over the curtains, the wallpaper, the spines of a few books. You can still see a few flecks over there. That isn't blood.'

'We aren't sure whether they'll be able to save the rug,' PG said glumly.

He knocked back the last of his whisky and then got to his feet, moving over to the bar cart to pour himself another. The ice clinked against the glass as he drank, still standing.

'He keeps a good pace,' Monika said drily.

'My tribute to Bellman,' PG replied, refilling his glass again before returning to his seat.

'I started dabbing at the rug with lukewarm water,' Monika continued. 'But there was so much port on it that I had to ask Amelie to come and help, even though it was five to eleven. The chairs, curtains and walls were all more or less OK, but the rug ... In the end we admitted defeat, rolled it up and carried it out to Amelie's car. It was ten to twelve by that point.'

'Five to eleven, ten to twelve – how can you be so sure about the timings?' asked Sid.

'On days when we have guests, like today, Amelie stays until eleven. I was afraid I might have missed her, so I remember checking the time,' Monika replied.

'And the other? Ten to twelve?'

'We have an alarm system here, you see, and it comes on automatically at midnight. Unless we actively disarm it, it's on until seven the next morning,' she explained.

'I only just made it back in time,' said PG.

'Surely you know the code?'

'I can't remember it even when I'm sober,' he said with a smile.

'I would just like to point out that this doesn't necessarily mean anything,' Monika spoke up, a flicker of weariness passing over her face.

'What doesn't?' asked Julia.

Monika sighed and sipped her grappa.

'Amelie and I were busy trying to lower the back seat of her car to make room for the rug when PG came wandering out of nowhere like some sort of ghost. I didn't think she was capable of it, but Amelie actually screamed ... We tried our best, but it was extremely hard to get PG to come inside. He was freezing cold and filthy, and he kept saying he wanted to see the stars ...'

'Top up, anyone? Sid?' asked PG.

'No, thank you.'

PG got up and filled his glass for the fourth time. He knocked it back in one go, poured himself another, then staggered back over to his armchair and slumped down. He blinked slowly a few times and closed both eyes. His face went slack, his mouth opening. Sid had just leapt up to catch the glass that was about to fall out of his hand when PG's eyes snapped open.

'Only kidding,' he said with a grin.

'God ...' Monika whispered.

'Sorry, Julia. Sorry, Sidney.'

'It's OK,' Sid said with a polite smile.

'Perhaps we should let our guests get some sleep?' Monika suggested.

'No, not yet. She thinks I've lost all sense of judgement, but it was just a joke,' PG explained, suddenly full of drunken energy. 'Let's keep going. I know you must have more questions for me. I'm not going to be able to sleep tonight, I should call the police and confess.'

'Don't say that,' Monika said in an attempt to reassure him.

'But I really can't bear it,' he mumbled.

'I know, my love, but we don't want to wear out our guests ...'

'You don't need to worry about us,' said Julia.

'OK, let's do this. PG, you have a glass of water. We'll finish our drinks and then call it a night,' said Monika.

Sid returned to his seat and lifted his glass from the table. PG moved back over to the bar cart and filled his glass with soda water.

'I'd like to know what you think might have happened. What possible motive could anyone have had to kill someone and then use PG's phone to take a picture of the body?' asked Sid.

'Assuming I didn't do it myself, you mean?' said PG, sitting back down.

'Yes.'

'Could it be a bad joke of some kind?' PG asked, wiping the sweat from his upper lip.

'In what sense?' Julia countered.

'In that no one is actually dead, that the picture was staged.'

'I'm pretty sure the man in the photograph really is dead,' said Sid.

Monika fiddled with her pearl necklace. 'This all just feels too absurd to be real,' she mumbled.

'What other possible motives can you think of?' asked Julia.

'Someone might have decided to kill someone and then framed PG for it, for one reason or another ... Though that feels a bit far-fetched,' said Monika.

'Or blackmail,' suggested PG.

'But you haven't received any demands for money, have you?' asked Julia.

'No.'

'They could be waiting until he's charged,' said Monika. 'If they're—'

'If they are then they clearly don't know me very well,' PG interrupted her.

'Go on, Monika,' said Sid. 'You were saying something.'

She shook her head, causing a lock of red hair to hang loose over her forehead.

'It wasn't important, I was just speculating ... Whoever did this could be waiting until PG is on the verge of being convicted before they come up with some kind of deal that would save him.'

'But who might do that? Are you thinking of anyone specific?'

'No,' she sighed. 'Everyone likes my husband.'

'Don't tease,' PG said with a smile.

'Have you really tried to identify the man in the photograph?' asked Sid.

'Yes,' PG mumbled.

'Have you looked closely, even though it's unpleasant?'

'I have.'

'It could be anyone,' said Monika.

Julia saw PG shake his head slightly, uttering another 'yes' that was little more than a sigh.

'You don't agree, do you, PG?' she said.

'I don't want to believe it, but it could be my brother Werther,' he replied.

'Is it Werther?'

'Forget what I said, it's impossible to tell,' he said, turning away.

'He's only saying that because Werther didn't appoint him as his proxy as usual,' Monika explained. 'And, as ever, we can't get hold of him.'

'We would be very grateful if you could keep trying,' said Julia.

'Sometimes it takes Werther months to get back to us,' PG spoke up.

'If we could return to the picture for a moment,' said Sid. 'Do you recognise where it was taken? The room, the floor?'

'No,' said PG.

'We'll be able to get a pretty precise location from the masts the phone communicated with, but it usually takes a little while to get that information.'

Amelie came into the room with a tray of clean glasses for the bar cart, hurrying away as quickly as she had appeared.

'You don't have any idea where it might be?' asked Julia.

'It's a cement floor and a brick wall ...' said PG. 'It could be anywhere.'

'If you ignore the time constraints, yes. But the photograph was taken at twenty-five past eleven, and the phone had to be back in the manor house before the alarm came on at twelve,' said Julia.

'Because we're the only ones with the code,' PG nodded.

'I don't understand,' said Monika, eyes darting between Julia and Sid.

'You think it was taken on the property?' asked PG.

# 8

Julia felt slightly woozy as she took off her dress, draped it over the back of a chair, unhooked her bra and put it on top. She then walked over to the dark window, where her reflection was transformed into that of a beautiful young woman in the wavy old glass.

She turned away, trying to swallow the lump in her throat as she opened the wardrobe and pulled on her silk slip. The fabric felt cool and feather-light against her skin.

Julia brushed aside all thoughts of why she had packed her prettiest underwear and went through to the bathroom, where she turned on both taps above the cracked hand basin, washed her face and looked up at the mirror. The water running down her cheek followed the groove of the scar before dripping from her chin.

She was thinking about the revelation that Monika and Amelie had been busy carrying the rug out to Amelie's car when they bumped into PG on his way back to the house, just before twelve.

Their conversation in the Red Room had gained momentum following the realisation that the photograph must have been taken somewhere on the property. Monika had got hung up on the idea that the dead man could be a forestry worker. He might have injured himself on a chainsaw, she said, and the rope around his wrists could be from his colleagues dragging him out of the woods, the sack over his head to cover his terrible injuries. They might have taken the picture on PG's phone in order to demand compensation for their dangerous working conditions. She had then trailed off and given a resigned shrug to show that not even she believed it, that she knew it was just a desperate attempt to protect her husband.

It was touching to see her try to find ways to clear her husband, thought Julia.

She dried her face and applied her night cream, then returned to her bedroom, turned out the bedside light and moved back over to the same spot by the window, peering out at the dark shapes outside through the bumpy glass.

There was a brief flash of orange light in the distance, and Julia leaned in to the window, felt the chill on her face.

The road and the trees looked like leaden marble against the dark sky.

She saw the same light again, a little further to the right this time, flickering somewhere between red and yellow. For whatever reason, it made her think of a young girl carrying red-hot coals on a copper plate.

She shuddered when she heard a knock at the door, and she moved back over to the bedside table and switched on the lamp. A shiver passed down her spine as she turned the key in the lock and opened the door.

'Can I come in?' asked Sid.

'Of course,' she replied, limping back over to the bed and sitting down on the edge of the mattress.

Sid followed her in and paused in the middle of the room. His phone pinged with a message, but he pretended not to have heard it.

'I just wanted to say that I managed to show Amelie the picture from PG's phone before she left for the evening,' he said.

'I wish you had waited until I was there, so I could read her response.'

'Sorry, I know, I just thought I might as well get it over and done with.'

'Typical cop,' she sighed, gesturing to the armchair.

'Sorry,' he said again, taking a seat.

'It's fine, just try to remember every detail.'

Sid nodded. 'I went to the linen cupboard with her to get an extra pillow and I asked if she could help me ... No, hang on, I said we needed help identifying someone, warned her that it might be upsetting.'

'OK,' said Julia. 'So you held up the photo on your phone, she looked at it, and then what?'

'She immediately turned away, went all pale. She didn't want to sit down, but—'

'You gave her some time?'

'Yes.'

'Did she shudder at any point?'

'I don't know.'

'Did you have to ask her again?'

'Yes, I repeated the question of whether she recognised the man in the picture.'

'And you thought it seemed like she did?'

'She said: "I hate to say it, but it almost looks like Werther ... I don't know, I don't want to get involved, but I understand the family can't get hold of him."'

'Were those her exact words?'

'I don't have your memory, but I think so,' Sid replied. 'She explained that they'd "been forced to make an interim decision at the AGM, given Werther didn't appoint a proxy as usual".'

'Interesting,' Julia said with a nod. 'And Monika's alibi?'

'She confirmed everything Monika told us. The port, the rug – she even remembered PG saying he wanted to look at the stars.'

'Did she look you in the eye as she said that?'

'Yes.'

'And right before, between the question and her answer?'

'She was busy trying to find a pillow case.'

'It's best to wait until you have eye contact with someone before you ask them a question,' she reminded him.

'I know, you've told me, but I forgot.'

Julia gave Sid a slight nod and took a deep breath.

'PG is the only person with three possible roles in this. Perpetrator, witness and victim,' she said.

'Sometimes I forget just how smart you are.'

'Though I'm like Jacques Brel ... I couldn't tell you what I'd give to be cute-cute for an hour, even in a stupid-ass way.'

'You are cute,' Sid said softly.

'Don't say that.'

'It's true,' he said, getting to his feet.

'Can I get you anything?' she asked. 'A nightcap?'

'No, I need to sleep,' he replied, giving her a weary smile.

'Good night,' Julia whispered.

Sid leaned in and kissed her forehead.

Julia took a deep breath and felt the touch of his lips surging across her face like a tidal wave, down her throat and out to her nipples.

The door closed behind him, and she waited a few seconds before getting up to turn the key, resting her forehead against the wood.

'*Meyn zis libhober*,' she whispered, making her way back over to the bed, lying down and closing her eyes.

It was the only Yiddish she had ever learned, but she had used it often. *My sweet love.*

She still couldn't quite believe she had let him down so badly.

Julia had had sex with other men both before and after Sid, but he was the only one who had ever managed to get past her trauma, who hadn't left her feeling like she wanted to die.

Perhaps that was down to his honesty, his incredible patience, or maybe it was simply because of his absolute presence in the moment whenever he touched her.

He managed to turn everything that sent her spiralling in panic at the slightest of touches on its head. Julia wasn't sure whether or not it was true, but she liked to tell herself that she had experienced more pleasure during her years with him than most people did in a lifetime.

Her right hand crept down between her legs, and she felt the weight, the heat, but the thought of masturbating was just too sad.

# 9

A CHILD IN A NAPPY WAS staring up at her, fingers in their mouth. Julia turned the other way and saw the blue sky like a shard of glass between the dark grey rocks.

She rolled over onto her side and forced the dream in another direction. A huge digger was busy filling in a pit, covering pale body parts with rocks, earth and torn roots.

A moment later, the sudden stench of burning flesh and diesel dragged her back to the surface, waking her up.

She stared out into the darkness. She was in bed, she realised, her breathing heavy. And she could smell smoke.

Without hesitating, she got up and moved over to the door, gingerly reaching out to touch the brass handle.

It was cold.

She opened the door. There was no sign of any smoke in the corridor, but she could hear quick footsteps and raised voices from the floor below.

Julia turned back into her room and drew the curtains. There was no need to open the window to see what was going on outside. Over by the lake, black smoke was billowing up into the pale dawn sky.

She pulled on her jacket over her nightie, grabbed her cane and went out into the corridor to knock on Sid's door.

'One second,' she heard him shout.

She knocked again and then started making her way towards the stairs. The door opened behind her, and Sid ran to catch up.

'Where's the fire?' he asked, tucking his shirt into his trousers.

'Somewhere over by the lake.'

'Do we think that's the scene of the murder?'

'Probably.'

They walked down the stairs and out through the front door, which was wide open. The air was thick with smoke, and Julia could hear sirens in the distance.

Monika and PG were already outside, hurrying over the gravel towards the water.

Sid and Julia set off after them.

Monika was wearing a fur coat, and her hair was messy. PG had on a pair of rubber boots, striped pyjama bottoms and a quilted jacket.

Julia thought back to the light she had seen before she went to bed. There was a chance it had nothing to do with any of this, but *someone* had definitely been moving about the property in the darkness.

The glow of the fire and the blue lights of the emergency vehicles flickered between the trunks as they raced along the gravel track.

Monika and PG turned off onto a smaller road through a cluster of trees. It took them down the edge of a field to the lake.

By the shore, a small building was ablaze, its roof completely engulfed. The flames had to be at least ten metres high, mixing with a column of black smoke. The windows had shattered in the heat, and the fire was licking up the brick walls. Firefighters in protective clothing were busy unwinding hoses from their vehicles, shouting commands to one another.

Monika and PG stopped when they reached the wall of heat, and Julia and Sid caught up with them.

'The brewhouse,' said Monika, gesturing wearily. 'The light from the fire woke me. PG called the emergency services, they got here in twenty-five minutes, but ...'

The heat felt oppressive on their faces, the smoke sharp and acrid.

Several trees close to the small building had now caught fire, and the flames hissed as the water sprayed over the building.

The fire and flashing blue lights glittered on the calm surface of Kvarnsjön, ash and burning embers sailing down through the air like light snowflakes.

PG watched on in disbelief as the firefighters worked. His white hair was standing on end.

'Are you OK?' Julia asked him.

'I'm so ashamed ... I feel responsible,' he said, turning to her. 'My father took such pride in every building, every outhouse and root cellar. He oiled any creaking hinges, polished the copper fixtures ...'

Julia met his bloodshot eyes and saw herself reflected in his pupils. With the bright glare behind him, he was nothing but a silhouette to her. Every slight shift in tone and rhythm seemed to grow in intensity, the falling flakes of soot slowing and the fury of the flames easing off slightly.

She felt the air being forced out of her lungs, as though she had just been hit in the gut. That was followed by a sensation of weightlessness, almost like she was floating, and the sound of the fire changed, dampened by the roar of the plane engines in the cabin.

'I think he must have counted virtually every tree in the area,' said PG, smiling to himself.

Everything went quiet, and the ash hovered motionless in the air. The fire froze like swaying crystals on a chandelier.

'He wasn't an affectionate man, he didn't have much love to give,' PG continued. 'But he did all this for his family. He gave us Mannheim, he gave us this ...'

As PG pointed at the fire, his hand slowly dropped to his side, shaking softly.

Monika said something in an anxious voice, and with that everything sped up again. The ash started swirling through the air, the roof collapsed with a roar, and sparks surged up into the night sky.

Julia and Sid moved back as PG shouted something to one of the firefighters, a despairing tone to his voice.

'Interesting,' said Julia.

'What, the fact that someone burnt down the old brewhouse?'

'No, that PG said his father gave them "this" and then pointed at the fire, the destruction.'

'Did he?'

'Subconsciously, yes.'

'How could I have missed that?'

'You're a cop. You see other things.'

'Julia, I'm trying to say that you never stop impressing me.'

'I'm damaged and unpleasant and—'

'Don't say that.'

After around 100 or so metres, they paused and turned around to watch the firefighters again. A hazy cloud of steam now hung above the overheated ground surrounding the burning house.

'You're quiet, Julia,' said Sid, hesitantly touching her arm. 'Everything OK?'

She looked up and met his kind eyes.

'You know how it is sometimes, when I meet new people ... I get the sense that they're about to disappear, that I'm witnessing their final moments,' she explained, leaning heavily on her cane.

'I thought that stuff had all got better?'

'I don't want it to get better.'

'You've always pushed yourself too hard, you know.'

'It's fine, I need this. I need the focus,' she replied, thinking about those moments when everything seemed to grind to a halt and she saw it as her duty to register and remember every last detail of things people said and did, and all because it felt as though she was hearing their final words.

# 10

MORNING ARRIVED LIKE A SOMBRE visitor, mercilessly laying bare the destruction. The firefighters had managed to put out the blaze, and the ground around the gutted building was drenched.

All that remained of the brewhouse was a heap of charred bricks and concrete. Steam was still rising from the warm ruins.

A sooty floor joist smouldered with a persistent high-pitched note.

A wheelbarrow had melted around a blackened tree trunk in a kind of embrace.

A fine layer of grey ash had settled over the flowers and grass.

PG put a comforting arm around Monika's shoulders as they made their way back towards the house.

No one could bring themselves to go back to bed, and so they gathered in the dining room instead.

Julia's throat felt raw from the smoke, and her eyes were still stinging.

On the other side of the window, she watched as the fire engines drove away.

Monika went through to the kitchen, and Julia followed her, pausing in the service corridor to watch as she chatted to

Amelie, who was frying bacon on the stove. A slight shiver passed over Amelie's face as the hot oil spat onto her hand. Without a word, Monika grabbed a small pot of salve from a cupboard and tenderly rubbed it into Amelie's skin before taping a dressing over the top.

Julia turned back into the dining room and took a seat beside Sidney. PG was nursing a mug of coffee in both hands, his nostrils black with soot from all the smoke he had inhaled.

'I had a quick word with the firefighters, but they said there was nothing that immediately jumped out at them,' Sid told her, coughing into his hand.

'Could they have missed a body?' Julia asked.

'No, I don't think so.'

Monika came back into the room with a cup of tea and a rusk on a saucer. She had been crying, her eyes puffy and her face grey with exhaustion.

'Do they know what started the fire?' she asked.

'There'll be an investigation, there always is,' Sidney replied in a husky voice. 'The first technicians usually arrive pretty quickly. I'm planning to go out and see what's happening in a little while.'

'Good,' Monika whispered.

'Could the picture of the body have been taken in the brewhouse?' asked Julia. 'Based on the floor and the brick walls.'

'Absolutely,' said PG. 'Though on the other hand we have rather a lot of buildings that look more or less the same ...'

'Still, considering the fire it seems pretty obvious it was there,' said Monika.

'It could all be a coincidence,' said Julia. 'Though we don't really believe that.'

'So the fire was started deliberately?' asked PG.

'Most likely,' said Julia.

'To destroy evidence?'

'The two of you being here has made someone nervous,' said Monika.

'*I'm* nervous, but that didn't make me set fire to my own house,' PG muttered.

'Were either of you outside last night? Before the fire?' asked Julia.

'What time?' Monika replied.

'I saw something strange just before one.'

'What was it?' asked Sid.

'A faint light down by the road ... a sort of wavering red glow.'

'At 1 a.m.?'

'Yes, just before.'

'Well, it wasn't us. We were both asleep then,' said Monika, turning to PG.

Without a word, Amelie came into the room and served three types of sandwich on sourdough bread: tuna mayonnaise, smoked ham and Dijon mustard, and Emmenthal with cherry tomatoes and fresh basil.

She turned back into the kitchen, reappearing a moment later with a large omelette packed with pepper, asparagus and celeriac, plus a plate of fruit and a jug of carrot and apple juice.

'You seem convinced that the murder happened here, on the property,' said PG. 'And that the image was taken by someone who was in the house – a member of the family, in other words.'

'Should we be worried?' asked Monika, helping herself to a piece of melon. 'I mean, should we go away somewhere or get bodyguards or whatever it is people do?'

'That sounds a bit over the top,' said PG.

'But it's no small thing to kill a person and burn down a building, is it? I'd never really considered that before now, that it could be dangerous for us to stay here.'

'Can you think of anyone who might pose a threat to you?' asked Sid.

'No, no idea. Some madman, a psychopath,' she replied.

'Do you know anyone you'd consider a psychopath?' asked Julia.

'This probably isn't the most warm and loving family in the world ...' PG spoke up.

'What?!' Monika asked with mock surprise.

'But we're not so bad,' he replied with a smile.

'None of the current generation have children – us included – which is ... quite interesting,' Monika said solemnly. 'It's as though everyone finally realised that no good will ever come from spreading the Mott family genes.'

PG got abruptly to his feet, wiped his mouth on his napkin and tossed it down onto his plate.

'I understand if you no longer feel like a guided tour today,' he said.

'On the contrary,' Julia replied.

'OK, then we'll stick to our plan,' he said, turning and walking away.

An uncomfortable silence settled over the room. Sid ate a few mouthfuls of omelette, and Julia finished off her tuna sandwich.

'Sorry about that, I can be a bit insensitive at times,' Monika sighed, lowering her cutlery. 'I'm really not the right person to cast the first stone.'

'We appreciate your honesty,' Julia told her.

'I'm not sure honesty is the right word. I can't stand myself when I'm cruel like that; it's just so unnecessary.'

'Has PG ever turned violent after drinking too much?'

Monika stared at Julia with a look of disbelief.

'Per Günter? He's the world's kindest man.'

Julia sipped her juice and gazed out through the window. A fine layer of ash had collected on the sill. She looked up at the sky above the treetops for a moment, then turned to the others.

'Monika, I know this might be a sensitive subject,' Julia began, 'but since you brought it up, I just have to ask: why haven't the two of you started a family?'

'What, considering PG is the world's kindest man?'

'Yes.'

Monika pursed her lips and turned to the window. It was as though her emotions had got the better of her. Her eyes began to well up, and she blinked repeatedly to force them back, trying to find her smile before she got to her feet and left the dining room.

# 11

The stench of smoke was overpowering as Julia came out onto the stone steps, and sluggish clouds of ash swirled around her feet she walked across the gravel and paused by the lawn in the middle of the turning circle. According to the sundial, it was almost nine. She leaned against her cane and gazed over towards the trees in front of the gutted building. Between the trunks, she could see Sidney chatting to two people in protective white clothing.

She was thinking about Monika's reaction to her question about why she and PG didn't have children. For a few seconds, it was as though she had lost control of her carefully crafted facade. She had also managed to escape without answering the question.

Julia replayed the entire conversation from breakfast in her mind, dwelling on the paradox – likely perfectly innocent – in Monika's claim that both she and PG had been asleep at 1 a.m. How could she possibly know that he had been sleeping if she was too, and vice versa?

When she turned back towards the brewhouse, Julia saw that Sid was making his way towards her. He waved and jogged the last few metres, pausing with a smile. She had to make a real effort to maintain a serious face.

'What do the technicians have to say?' she asked.
'Not much.'
'But you were talking to them.'
'As a private individual, yes.'
'So they didn't tell you anything?'
'They're not allowed.'
'Oh, come on,' Julia sighed.
'But I did see that they were using nylon evidence bags,' he said.
'You know forensics isn't my strongest subject.'
'They only tend to do that when they want to collect flammable liquids.'
'Shouldn't they have burned off?' she asked.
'You might think so, but it's actually pretty common for the technicians to find traces of accelerant after a fire,' he explained.
'OK ...'
'Take petrol, for example. It consists of over 500 hydrocarbons, and the most volatile of them burn off in a flash. But when it comes to the less volatile ones ... traces of those can hang around. If, for example, they've soaked into something before the match is struck.'

A Land Rover was approaching the manor house along the gravel track.

'So what you're trying to say is that the use of these nylon evidence bags suggests they think some sort of accelerant was used to start the fire?'
'And that whoever did it wasn't taking any risks – they wanted everything to go up in flames, presumably because the evidence was so damning, it outweighed the attention a fire would bring.'
'Bravo, Sid. Maybe you're not just a pretty face after all.'

# I WILL FIND THE KEY

The Land Rover swung around the turning circle, crunching over the gravel and pulling up in front of them. The driver's side door opened and PG climbed out, dropping his phone into the inner pocket of his green hunting waistcoat.

'I thought I'd drive you to lunch after our guided tour,' he said.

'Perfect, thanks,' Sid replied.

'I've been standing out here for a while now, taking in the manor house,' said Julia. 'It's all so beautiful, with the forest and the little lake.'

'And on the other side of the dam, you can see the river, the remains of the old watermill and the chapel,' PG told her, pointing.

'What I'm wondering is ... how do you see the future of all this?' she asked.

'The future,' PG repeated with a sigh. 'Well, I suppose we're just eating a late supper on the upper deck as the ship sinks.'

'Is that so?' Julia smiled.

'Yes, probably,' he said with a shrug.

'So what went wrong?'

'I don't know, but the first-born men in the family devoted all their time and energy to the company. They started families late in life. The company was passed down from father to son – Mannheim, Leopold and Sylvester ... ending up with Werther.'

'Who doesn't have any children.'

PG mumbled something inaudible and got back into the driving seat. Julia climbed in beside him, propping her cane between her knees and closing the door.

They set off the minute Sid was in the back, rolling slowly around the turning circle and pulling out onto the smaller road off to one side of the avenue of trees.

The ragged trees were mirrored in the calm surface of the lake, and Julia noticed veils of white smoke rising from the charred remains of the brewhouse. The ground around it was still drenched following the fire fighters' efforts to extinguish the blaze, and the two technicians Sid had spoken to were busy taking off their white overalls behind their van.

'My family has always worked in these forests,' PG began. 'Chopping, sawing, planing, log driving ... Damn hard work.'

As he drove, he tried to explain the Mannheim Group's success as a combination of luck and a good eye for business. During the first half of the nineteenth century, many of Europe's forests had been wiped out as a result of rapid industrialisation, but Sweden's natural resources remained largely untapped.

'That was the single most important factor enabling my great grandfather Mannheim to exploit the situation. His father was the foreman of a water-powered sawmill, which meant he was able to send young Mannheim to Stockholm for an education,' PG continued.

Having completed an apprenticeship in England, Mannheim returned to Sundsvall and started Sweden's very first steam-powered sawmill in Tunadal in the winter of 1849.

'The timing was perfect.'

Parliament had just passed a law making it easier for industrialists to acquire capital, and Mannheim Mott was able to buy up forest to secure the logging rights. By the end of the century, he was Sweden's second richest man after Alfred Nobel.

'But my great grandfather wasn't the only one,' PG hastened to add. 'The logging industry expanded in a kind of pyramid. Many businessmen became extremely wealthy over the course of just a few decades.'

'A completely new upper class,' said Julia.

'Which inevitably led to accusations of dubious business practices, illegal felling and poor taste – all of which made it especially important for a family like ours to steer clear of any extravagances or scandals.'

'Of course,' Julia nodded.

'I don't know, maybe it's an inferiority complex or whatever you want to call it, but I always think that the dirt throwing and disparaging names like "logging baron" were the nobility's way of trying to cling on to power by creating a hatred of new money.'

'Which is now seen as old money,' she pointed out.

'The financial crashes took the lion's share of our wealth. We're far from being the country's richest family today, but nor are we scraping the barrel.'

The gravel track ran parallel to the river, following the sweeping bends in the silvery water. After around three kilometres, Julia spotted two red houses by the shore.

'The bigger of the two,' said PG, slowing down slightly, 'was Augustus's house at one point in time. My father's cousin. Björn and André grew up there, and now they share it – they have a floor each ... though André often stays at his girlfriend's place.'

'And the other?'

'That belongs to their younger sister, Siri.'

'What does she do for a living?' asked Sidney.

'Some sort of physical therapy for children with special needs, if I've understood it correctly,' PG replied, speeding up again.

'We'd like to talk to her, if we could,' said Julia.

'It's all arranged.'

'Thank you.'

'I've been thinking about this business with my phone,' PG spoke up after a while. 'Couldn't it be that I heard a noise and went down to the brewhouse, saw the dead man and didn't know what to do, so I took a picture, planning to call the police ... and then forgot all about it on my way back?'

'The thought did cross my mind,' said Julia. 'But the fact that you would have had to put your phone back where you left it before you went to bed makes it seem unlikely.'

'I usually put it there during dinner to avoid being interrupted, but when I go to bed it's always on the nightstand ... I don't know, I was incredibly drunk, I might have got my times mixed up and thought it was day even though it was the middle of the night.'

After around twenty minutes, they turned off onto the old logging road that led to various felling sites in the forest.

'We currently have a little more than 400,000 hectares of land,' PG explained as they bounced along the uneven terrain. 'The quality is fantastic, probably the best in Västernorrland. The trees are even-aged, and we have areas of thinning and planting.'

The tall trunks flickered by, and they passed a storage area with huge stacks of logs, muddy ground and a stationary forwarder.

'Have you ever been violent during one of your blackouts?' asked Julia.

'You've already asked me that,' PG replied, giving her a sideways glance.

'And I need you to take the question seriously.'

'Monika says I often get agitated, that she's had to stop me from doing silly things.'

'Such as?'

'I tried to climb onto the roof of the manor house last winter, despite the fact that I could barely stand.'

'But she stopped you?'

They could hear the first saws now, and after another ten minutes they reached a logging area.

'We make use of everything – twigs, stumps, branches,' PG explained as he brought the car to a halt.

Through the windscreen, they watched as a cascade of wood shavings sprayed through the air. A harvester gripped a tree in its claw, sawed through the trunk and sliced it into three logs in the space of just a few seconds.

'You left the table when Monika mentioned that there are no children in the family,' said Julia.

'I think that's a private matter.'

'It is,' she nodded.

PG sighed and turned to look at her. 'I don't want children. I can barely take care of myself, and now it turns out I might have murdered a man.'

'But Monika was talking about the Mott genes.'

'Nature or nurture, it doesn't really make any difference to us; the two are welded together,' PG said cryptically before getting out of the car.

They watched him stride across the logging area towards the harvester. Bark and twigs swirled around the enormous machine as trunks were split and thudded to the ground. Another tree toppled, dry woodchips flying.

PG whistled, and the enormous harvester fell silent. The driver climbed down from the cab and walked over to him, shook his hand. He then took off his helmet and smiled. PG pointed to the edge of the forest and said something. The driver nodded, and they started walking away.

Julia watched them disappear behind the trees. She couldn't stop thinking about what PG had said about his father having counted every tree in the area, having taken care of Mannheim down to the very last detail. Despite that, he had handed thirty per cent of the company to his cousin Augustus. Why? It was a question she planned to save until the opportune moment, possibly that evening, when they all gathered for dinner.

But before that they were due to meet Björn, the eldest of the second cousins.

Julia couldn't help but smile. The investigation was finally underway, and it wouldn't be long until the pieces started to fall into place.

# 12

Square meal, the restaurant where they had arranged to meet Björn, was on the outskirts of Sundsvall. It was a small place, with checked tablecloths and real carnations in vases.

PG had dropped them off on his way to a meeting with the Stora Enso Group about the latest EU regulations on the management of ancient forest.

It was still early, and the restaurant was empty as Julia and Sid stepped inside. Björn Mott hadn't arrived. A young woman with rosy cheeks showed them to a table, brought over a jug of water and handed them both a menu.

Julia wanted to meet the three cousins separately before she saw them all together and with PG and Monika. There was almost nothing that gave a person a better understanding of someone than observing them and paying close attention to the shifting dynamic as the company around them changed.

'Mannheim, though ... What a place,' said Sid. 'Totally over the top, but ...'

'Incredible, isn't it?'

'But ... we've only been here one night, and I already feel a bit claustrophobic.'

'I don't know, there's something about their inheritance,' said Julia, stretching her leg beneath the table. 'They love to moan about this clause that forces them to sit down together once a week, but they're also a bit like wasps – they just can't help but go back to the glass.'

'Sugar for everyone,' he grinned.

'And yet they all hate each other.'

A blue minibus from the mobility service pulled up on the street outside. The driver opened the rear doors and unfolded a ramp. He climbed it, disappearing briefly, and re-emerged a moment later, pushing a man in an electric wheelchair.

The waitress hurried over to hold the door open as the man in the wheelchair reversed into the restaurant. He pushed the joystick in the other direction and spun around.

Björn Mott was like a plump, slightly neglected version of PG, with an unhappy furrow on his forehead, baggy jeans and a navy flannel shirt.

Moving impatiently, awkwardly, he came towards them in his sky blue wheelchair with faux leather armrests and a red reflector on the back. The safety belt was hanging loose at one side, and the small front wheels squeaked.

Julia got up, gripping her cane in order to get out of shaking his hand.

'I'm Julia Stark, and this is my colleague Sidney,' she said, gesturing to him with her cane.

'Expected someone a bit sterner, with a name like Stark,' Björn sighed, knocking against the table and making the jug shake, spilling water onto the tablecloth.

'Thank you for coming to see us at such short notice,' said Sid, shaking his hand.

Björn gave them both a strained smile, lifted his armrests and rolled closer to the table before applying the brake.

'PG said you wanted to ask a few questions and treat me to lunch?'

'Yes, we—'

'You ask, I'll eat and drink,' he interrupted her, rapping his knuckles on the table.

The waitress came over with a menu, and Björn used his hand to cover his glass as she lifted the jug of water.

'I'll have a pint of your strongest beer, two Jägermeisters and a glass of Fernet,' he said, turning to Julia with a smile. 'A man's got to keep up appearances, just like my brother does when he pretends to read Shakespeare when his fancy clients come to visit.'

'Anything to eat?' the waitress asked.

'Right. I'll have the hash. Four eggs, no beetroot.'

She nodded and then turned to Sid and Julia.

'How's the fish stew?' asked Sid.

'Very good, nice and herby. Served with sugar snap peas, aioli and sourdough.'

'Perfect.'

'I'll go for the same,' said Julia.

'And to drink?'

'Water is fine, thanks.'

Björn studied them with glassy, bloodshot eyes.

'You're from Stockholm, I get it,' he said. 'Everywhere you turn, all you see is forest. But me, I see every single tree. The quality, the tone ... As timber, roof trusses, part of a cabinet, slow-growing spruces, tall pines ... Birch root, willow ... But you don't care about any of that.'

'We understand you restore antique furniture?' Julia began.

'Doesn't take a super sleuth to work that one out,' he replied with a grin.

'No.'

'Sorry for asking, but how old are you?'

'Is that relevant?' Julia shot back.

'You look good, despite this thing,' he said, trailing a finger down his cheek.

'Have you heard that the brewhouse burnt down last night?' she asked, ignoring him. 'That was where you stored some of your things, wasn't it?'

'Yeah, it's a bloody shame,' Björn sighed, pushing his hair back from his face. 'I had some really nice Rococo stuff in there. Priceless pieces, things from Sylvester and Leopold's day. The insurance won't cover even a fraction of it.'

'It must take real skill, your work,' said Julia. 'I'm thinking of all the elaborate intarsia and—'

'Intarsia's easy,' said Björn, pressing his rough fingers against the table. 'It's the accidental damage that takes time. Like when some idiot has been keeping pot plants on a lacquered table and you have to bleach the stains and relacquer the whole thing, gently waxing the surface until—'

The waitress came over with Björn's drinks, and he knocked back the glass of Fernet-Branca and returned it to her tray before she even had time to turn around.

'It was the shareholders' meeting on Sunday,' said Julia. 'Did anything unusual happen?'

Björn shrugged.

'Ask a wheel what it thought of the last loop,' he said, taking a few deep swigs of beer.

'It's a big company. Decisions are made at these meetings.'

'New meeting, same old shit. Year after year. There's only ever one question: should we keep hold of Mannheim or not? Everyone knows which way it's going to go, but we still have to vote ... The three of us want to sell, but Werther, that stuck-up bastard, he likes having the family under his heel. He can't even be bothered to show up any more, just appoints his little brother to be his proxy and then PG votes exactly as he's told.'

Björn positioned his two Jägermeisters so that they were in a perfect line with his beer glass.

'You don't seem to like Werther much,' said Julia.

'No one does.'

'Why is that?'

'There's nothing to like, the man's a pig ... A liar, too. He was actually supposed to show up for once on Sunday, but he didn't in the end. Am I surprised? No.'

Björn gave a thumbs-down and knocked back one of the shots.

'Do you know why he was planning to attend this time?'

'You'll have to ask him.'

The waitress came over with their food. She said 'bon appétit,' and they thanked her and picked up their cutlery.

'So nothing unusual happened at the meeting?' Julia pressed Björn, tearing off a piece of bread. 'Everything was like normal?'

'Everything was like normal,' he confirmed, leaning over his plate and shovelling hash into his mouth.

'What about the dinner afterwards?'

'Same,' he replied, his mouth full.

'What did you do later that evening, after dinner?' Sid asked.

Björn fixed his heavy eyes on him. 'I sat in the Red Room with my pal Johnnie Walker, lamenting my fate,' he replied sarcastically.

'And roughly what time was it when you got home?'

'They want everyone out of the castle before the carriage turns back into a pumpkin,' he said, patting his wheelchair.

'What time did you leave Mannheim?' asked Julia.

'The little hand was on eleven and the big one on two.'

'Did you see anyone else on your way home?'

Björn didn't seem to understand her question, and he simply shook his head and kept eating. He downed his third shot, finished off his beer and shouted for another.

'Did you cross paths with anyone on your way home?'

'What the hell's going on here?'

He quickly finished his food and pushed the empty plate away. Sid took out his phone and held up the photograph of the dead man. Björn sighed, leaned forward and squinted at the screen.

'Is that me?' he asked.

'Take a good look,' said Sid, enlarging the image.

'Someone's gone and got themselves killed and you're asking me ... what, exactly?'

'Whether you recognise him,' said Julia.

'He's got a fucking bag on his head. Am I the only one who can see that?'

'So you don't recognise him?'

'Should I?'

'When did you last speak to Werther?'

'You're kidding? Is that him? It can't be. Let me see again,' he said, gesturing impatiently at Sid.

Björn studied the image and shook his head.

'Why don't you like Werther?' asked Julia.

'I don't like anyone.'

'OK, but if we focus specifically on Werther for a moment,' she said, lowering her cutlery.

'Werther's eleven years older than me, but what a goddamn ... I had to keep an eye on him the whole time,' Björn replied, jabbing a finger towards his temple. 'We were only kids, but we could tell. There was something wrong with him. He was always so fucking interested in us, too. Wanted to wrestle with me, peep at my sister ... And he liked humiliating André.'

'In what sense?'

'Ask my little brother about oink oink,' he said, grabbing his next beer from the waitress as she approached.

'But you're all adults now, and you—'

'He's still the same sadist he was when we were little. He's the reason I ended up in this thing five years ago,' Björn interrupted her, patting his wheelchair again. 'Picked me up with a harvester because I had opinions about the accounts.'

'What happened?' asked Sid.

'Look, I don't mind a bit of messing about,' he replied with a dark smile. 'But a harvester's a fucking big machine, with a claw and sawblade.'

'We know.'

'Christ, I thought he was going to cut me in half.'

'So you injured your leg or—'

'My back,' he interjected, wiping the beer froth from his upper lip.

'OK.'

'Have to wear this brace now, a bit like one of those corsets women used to wear,' he explained, opening his shirt and tapping the hard plastic underneath. 'Really bloody uncomfortable, but they tell me I could end up paralysed if I don't wear it.'

'Did you report him to the police?' asked Sid.

'What difference would that have made?' Björn replied with a sigh, draining his beer.

# 13

SID AND JULIA WALKED SLOWLY away from the restaurant in the warm late summer air. They had helped Björn out to the waiting vehicle after lunch, and were now making their way over to André's shop on Esplanaden.

A bus pulled out from the kerb in a cloud of exhaust fumes.

Julia glanced over at Sid, wondering what he thought about being a private detective, how he felt about spending time with her again.

'The red light you saw last night, could it have been the reflector on Björn's wheelchair?' asked Sid.

'It has a reflector?'

'Several. Red at the back and orange on the wheels,' he replied.

'If you keep this up, you'll have earned your wage soon,' she said with a wry smile.

'The sharpest knife in the drawer, me,' he said with a reserved victory gesture.

They walked slowly across the square, the rubber foot of Julia's cane thudding softly against the paving stones. A flock of pigeons flapped up into the sky, feathers rustling.

'Björn might have been out and about last night, but he didn't take PG's phone,' said Julia. 'He wouldn't be able to get into the service corridor in his wheelchair. I guess they forgot to take people with mobility issues into consideration when they built the manor.'

She and Sid walked down the avenue of trees between the two sides of the road on Esplanaden. Dust swirled up from the gravel underfoot.

'It's beautiful here,' said Sid.

'The Stone City,' Julia mumbled, reaching up to adjust her uncomfortable bra straps.

She had read that large parts of Sundsvall were destroyed in a fire in 1888, and that they had decided to rebuild the city using stone – despite the fact that this was the golden age of the forestry magnate – in order to prevent anything similar from happening again.

The sound of her cane echoed dully between the facades. She glanced up at Sid's face in profile and thought back to the minutes before their wedding, when his fingers had trembled as he lowered the veil over her face.

Julia knew that he really had loved her then.

She listened to his footsteps alongside hers now and started to think about everything she had done to him.

Their divorce had been inevitable, silent and resolute.

Her breathing grew laboured, and she tried to force back the memories, to remind herself that, despite everything, he was still by her side.

Sidney had said that he didn't hate her, that he never had. And he continued to send her red roses on her birthday every year, to call.

It had been a long time since she had last picked up and let him come over to comfort her, because she knew he would always leave again. But she now had a plan: she would win back one small part of him, the police officer, and she would do so without allowing herself to get her hopes up. Because the truth was that she would never be able to reopen the box where his heart lived, no matter how desperately she wished she could.

They crossed the road and made their way over to a large window with the words *André Mott Antiques* painted on the glass. There was an old Porsche Cayman parked right outside, the name MOTT on its registration plate.

The spacious shop was full of display cases, desks, floor lamps, dark dining tables, varnished chairs, busts and ottomans. Countless chandeliers hung from the ceiling, and the walls were covered in sconces, mirrors and paintings of battlefields in golden frames. The air smelled like old leather and wood, like dusty fabric, paraffin and furniture polish.

A door opened to the rear, and a smiling man with a phone to his ear came towards them.

Julia had no doubt at all that this was André. He had the same eyes and the same dimpled chin as his brother, but his hair was darker, his nose more prominent. He was also slimmer and better dressed, in a relaxed kind of way.

'Yes, I have a customer who has shown an interest,' he said to whoever was on the other end of the line. 'But I'm afraid I'll have to ask you for a new certificate … Yes, I know you brought it with you, but it isn't here … Are you sure you didn't accidentally take it away with you? OK, I'm sorry, but—'

His call ended, and André shrugged and turned to them.

'Hi,' said Julia. 'I'm Julia Stark and—'

'Ah, of course. PG called. Julia and Sidney.' André was beaming. He hesitated for a moment when he noticed the scar on Julia's face, but then he held out a hand to greet them both.

'Could we take a seat somewhere?' Julia asked, gripping her cane tightly with both hands. 'I'm having a little trouble with my legs.'

'Of course, come through to my office.'

They followed him into the room at the rear of the shop. Behind the dusty computer and the thick folders on his desk, there was a cracked window looking out onto a paved courtyard.

Julia walked straight over to the bookshelf and pulled out a thick volume of Shakespeare's tragedies. She then opened the book and handed André the missing certificate.

'That's unbelievable,' he said, fanning himself. 'Absolutely incredible ...'

'A party trick.'

'Seriously though ... How the hell did you do that? I need to know.'

'Your brother mentioned that you often pretend to be reading Shakespeare when you have an important client, and I realised you might not have remembered that the certificate was tucked inside the book when you put it back after the meeting.'

'Still ... that's pretty bloody impressive,' said André.

They sat down on the handsome Carl Malmsten couch.

'Coffee?' André asked, giving Julia a flirty look.

'In a little while, please,' Julia replied, stretching out her legs with a sigh.

'So, I take it you've just come from lunch with my brother, that little ray of sunshine? I hope he didn't get drunk and silly?'

'No, it was fairly relaxed,' said Sid.

'He's a little sensitive at the moment. In quite bad shape, in fact, but he is a good person ... And a supremely gifted craftsman.'

'We understand you own this business together?'

'He does the work and I get paid,' André replied with a smirk.

'Is it going well?'

'Well, it's not going to make us rich, but we've found our niche, and that's definitely worth something.'

'I agree,' said Julia.

'We need to ask you a few questions,' said Sid.

'PG mentioned that you were investigating a photograph of a dead man ... ?'

Sid held up the image on his phone. André looked away almost immediately, as though he had just been given an electric shock.

'Christ, that's awful,' he said with a grin.

'Do you recognise the man?' asked Julia.

'Can't say I do, but you think it's Werther, don't you?'

'Yes.'

'In the brewhouse, which burnt down.'

'You seem sure,' said Sid.

'I'm guessing.'

'Your brother said that Werther was planning to attend the shareholders' meeting on Sunday,' Sid continued.

For the first time, André's smile faltered. He seemed genuinely taken aback.

'Werther? What gave him that idea?'

'When did you last see Werther?' Julia asked.

'God, it must've been Siri's birthday, September last year ... It's kind of a tradition for him to turn up with a huge bouquet and—'

'You killed him, didn't you?' Julia cut him off.

'You're kidding?' André was smiling again, but his eyes seemed anxious.

Julia's heart began pounding, so hard that she could hear the blood in her ears. She leaned in closer and fixed her eyes on André.

'I think—'

'Julia,' Sid spoke up, his voice calm.

'I haven't killed anyone,' said André.

'It was just a question,' she said, feeling her heart rate return to normal.

'Quite an insensitive one.'

'I'm sorry.'

'I'll forgive you ... because you found the certificate.'

'What did you do after the meeting on Sunday?' asked Sid.

André pursed his lips.

'We had dinner, everyone was there. Well, other than Werther, obviously ...'

'And did anything out of the ordinary happen?'

'Nope, it was the same as ever.'

'What does that mean?' asked Julia.

'We all ate and drank as though we had an appointment with the electric chair.'

'And after dinner?'

'Björn wanted to sulk in a corner with a bottle of whisky, and I had a grappa with my sister.'

'What about PG and Monika?'

'Same old, same old ... She was trying to get him to take it easy with the booze without causing a scene.'

'How long did you stay?'

'Siri'd had another big argument with Monika earlier that day, so she wasn't in the best of moods ... I don't know, I probably gave up after an hour or so, then I caught a cab over to my girlfriend Frida's place.'

'What time was it when you arrived at Frida's?'

'Twenty to twelve. We had a quick snack and listened to the news on the radio – you know, the broadcast just before midnight.'

'Do you remember what they were talking about?'

'No idea,' he replied with a grin.

'And what happened after the news?'

'I stayed over and then went to work as normal the next morning.'

'Could you send me Frida's details?' asked Julia.

'Of course,' said André, picking up his phone.

She studied him as he scrolled through his contacts, taking in his bloodshot eyes, the pale scar on the tip of his chin, his well-tended nails.

'Björn mentioned that you and he have wanted to sell Mannheim for some time?' she said after a moment.

'Yeah, but it's a bit of a deadlock ... I mean, I can understand PG and Monika, they live there, they manage the business – which is still turning a profit, even if the margins are shrinking.'

'And Werther?'

'He had a hard time with the order of sussess ... Christ, I can't even talk properly,' André grinned. 'Werther had a hard time with the order of *succession*, so he left.'

'Even though he benefited from it?'

'Yeah, but the price of that was his freedom. He didn't choose the role himself; it didn't suit him. I think it was actually Linnea, his mother, who sowed the seeds of his rebellion. She couldn't quite adapt to the Mott family traditions either, the role of a woman.'

'And what role is that?'

'Popping out babies ... full stop,' he said. 'Mannheim has been a prison for plenty of people.'

'Does that apply to you, Björn and Siri?'

'I mean, we're slightly removed from the worst of it, but sure. The place is nothing but trouble.'

'For all three of you?'

'I'd say so, yes.'

'Björn hates Werther,' said Julia.

'Did he tell you about the harvester?'

'Yes, but his feelings seem to predate that.'

'God, yes.'

'What about you? Do you hate Werther too?'

'Not enough to kill him, if that's what you're getting at.'

'Tell us about oink oink,' said Julia.

'Uff,' André replied, running a hand through his wavy hair. 'Yes, I can see Björn was really in his element earlier ... If we were growing up now, I'm sure Werther would've been slapped with all sorts of diagnoses – he probably would have been taken into protective custody or whatever it's called. But back then, people's parents didn't care what their children got up to. We were just left alone with the older kids, even if they were dangerous, damaged ...'

'So what happened?'

'It wasn't a big deal,' he said, still smiling. 'I was just so small, which made me an easy target.'

'What did he do?'

'He liked to humiliate me, a little kid,' he said.

'Why are you smiling?' asked Julia.

'I don't know, it's nothing to smile about,' said André. His eyes seemed to be welling up.

'What happened?' Julia pressed him.

'When I was four, Werther was sixteen.'

'That's a pretty big gap.'

'Yes,' he whispered.

Tears spilled down his cheeks, dripping onto the table. Sid seemed uncomfortable, and he rubbed his mouth.

'You said he humiliated you,' said Julia.

'It doesn't matter anymore, but it's still difficult to think about,' André explained, drying his cheeks. 'He had a fishing rod, and he tied the line around my dick and dragged me around ... He thought it was so funny to make me grunt like a pig and do all sorts of degrading things.'

'Like what?' asked Julia.

'You don't have to tell us,' said Sid.

'Sorry,' André mumbled, hurrying away with his hand over his mouth.

# 14

The bell above the door jingled as they left the shop and started making their way along the street in the bright sunlight.

'He who overcomes all dangers,' said Sid. 'Who passes all doors and—'

'Are you deliberately trying to mess things up, or what the hell's your problem?' Julia interrupted him.

Sid stopped and gave her a confused look.

'What have I done now?' he asked.

'Go home if you can't handle the job.'

'I can hear that you're angry, but I really don't know what—'

'I'm angry because people always protect men, because it's apparently so much more sensitive if a man has been degraded, abused or whatever.'

'You're right.'

'If it's a woman involved, she has to share every last detail. Her body becomes public fucking property, but if it's a man? Well, he has to be protected at any cost.'

'I'm sorry for—'

'You interrupted my interview and let him get away before I was done.'

'It was a mistake, Julia. I'm sorry about that. It was unintentional,' he said. 'A bit like when you rashly accused André of murder.'

'Yes, I got that wrong,' she mumbled, setting off again.

She was still agitated when she announced that she wanted to talk to André's girlfriend and called the number he had given her.

It rang and rang, and Julia imagined a phone in an empty room in an empty apartment. There was something about the way André had talked about Frida that made it seem like his girlfriend didn't even exist.

'Hello?' a husky voice eventually answered.

'Is that Frida?'

'Who's asking?'

'My name is Julia Stark, I'm currently investigating a matter on behalf of Per Günter Mott, André Mott's second cousin.'

'OK ...'

'We'd like to have a chat with you, if that's possible?'

'I was actually about to head out.'

'It'll only take five minutes. We're just outside André's shop. Are you at home?'

'Cross the square, in the direction of the water. Rådhusgatan 17, first floor.'


André's girlfriend lived in one of the handsome stone buildings in the city centre, with elaborate window frames and a copper roof.

Sid held the heavy door for Julia, and they stepped into the cool entrance hall and climbed the marble stairs.

The door to the apartment opened the minute they rang the buzzer. Frida was a tall woman in her thirties, with narrow eyes and a thin face. She was wearing a fringed leather jacket, tight-fitting jeans and a pair of cowboy boots with a Cuban heel.

'Who'd you say you were again?' she asked.

Julia took out her licence and held it up. 'We're private detectives, and we've been hired by a member of the Mott family to investigate a few events surrounding the recent AGM.'

'OK, but what does that have to do with me?'

Julia took a step forward in an attempt to force Frida back. It worked. She reluctantly moved to one side to make space for them in the hallway.

'Did you see André on Sunday?' asked Julia.

'Yeah, he came over here around ... half two.'

'In the afternoon?'

'Yes,' she replied with a smile.

'And how long did he stay?'

'I don't know. We had a coffee. An hour, maybe a little longer.'

'What did you do later that evening?'

'On Sunday? I was at the Royal,' she replied.

'What's that?'

'It's just a place. I dance there sometimes.'

'When did you get home?'

Frida thought for a moment, chewing her lip. It was unconscious, something she had probably done since she was a girl.

'I remember that I finished earlier than usual because there weren't many guests.'

'What time did you get home?'

'Eleven, maybe. Look, what's this about?'
'You're André Mott's girlfriend, aren't you?' asked Sid.
'Is that what he said?'
'Yes.'
Frida sighed. 'OK.'
'How would you describe your relationship?'
'We're friends.'
'Have you ever been anything other than that?'
'You guys really seem interested in our relationship,' she said.
'Maybe.'
'We party together, watch films. Eat, talk,' said Frida. 'Sometimes he slips a bit of money into my coat pocket when he knows I'm struggling. I don't know, he's just a really good friend …'
'OK.' Sid nodded.
'André says he slept over here on Sunday,' said Julia. 'Is that true?'
Frida met her eye without missing a beat. 'Yes.'
'What did you do when he arrived?'
'I was asleep. He rang the buzzer and woke me, and then I let him in,' she said, stifling a yawn.
'Did you have a bite to eat together, listen to the news?' asked Sid.
'Is that what he said?'
'We're asking you.'
'I honestly don't remember,' Frida replied, her face blank.
'Did he arrive at midnight?' asked Julia, looking her straight in the eye.
'Yes.'
'Not one?'

She shrugged.

'Two?'

'For God's sake, I was asleep,' she sighed.

'So you aren't sure?'

'I'm sorry, but I really have to go now,' she said, fishing her keys out of her bag.

\* \* \*

Julia leaned back in her seat during the taxi ride to Mannheim. She closed her eyes, thinking about the fact that André was only three when PG and Werther's mother Linnea died. There was no way he could have known from first-hand experience that she had struggled to adapt to her role within the Mott family.

Sid was chatting to the driver, trying to start a conversation about the Motts by talking about the importance of the forestry magnates to Sundsvall, but all he got was a bitter remark about the 1931 shooting in Ådalen, when five people were killed after police opened fire on striking workers from the pulp factory there.

They then sat in silence as the tall, straight pines raced hypnotically by on both sides of the car.

Twenty-two kilometres later, they passed through the tall iron gates at the edge of the Mannheim estate and the landscape opened out around them as though they had just emerged from a dark tunnel. Expanses of grass in the sunshine, the airy avenue of trees leading to the manor house, the glittering surface of the lake.

'There was a fire here last night,' Sid said as they passed the charred remains of brewhouse.

'All empires crumble and die eventually,' said the driver. 'And the first sign usually goes by the name of Caligula or Cleopatra ...'

He trailed off to fiddle with the meter as they drove down the avenue and approached the house. The sunlight over the treetops made the windows shimmer like opals.

The car rolled around the turning circle and pulled up by the front door. As Sid paid and asked for a receipt, Julia unfastened her seatbelt, grabbed her cane and got out. There was still a hint of smoke in the air, and she could hear the roar of a chainsaw in the distance.

Sid closed the car door and took Julia's arm as they climbed the steps. He held the door open for her, and they made their way into the grand entrance hall. There was a vase of white roses on a table by the mirror, and the fire in the hearth was crackling, casting a warm glow over the floor and ceiling.

The soft sound of music drifted out from the drawing room, and they followed it in and saw a woman sitting at the grand piano, playing Brahms's Piano Sonata No. 3. On the lid of the piano, beside the music stand, there was a scratched platinum ring set with a large diamond.

Julia moved over the rug without a sound, enabling her to study the woman's face in profile from behind. It was Siri, who had promised to meet them for a chat before dinner.

Her bright blonde hair spilled down over her bare shoulders. She was slim, wearing a delicate beige dress with thin straps, and the muscles in her slender arms worked as her fingers danced across the keys.

Siri possessed an old-fashioned, romantic kind of beauty, and the fine lines around her eyes and on her forehead gave her an attractive depth.

Once again, Julia found herself thinking about the fact that PG's father had, for some reason, given thirty per cent of Mannheim to his cousin Augustus. As a result of that, Siri now owned ten per cent of the company, enabling her to sit here playing the piano with a sense of belonging.

The ring by the music stand vibrated softly on the low notes.

As the tune came to an end, Julia and Sid both clapped. Siri got up and turned around with a smile.

'This is where I'm supposed to pretend I didn't hear you come in, isn't it?' she said, bowing slightly.

Her big eyes glittered in the sunlight flooding in through the window. Her cheeks were flushed, and her lips surprisingly full.

'That was incredible,' said Sid.

It seemed to take every ounce of Siri's strength not to let her smile falter when she noticed the long scar on Julia's face.

'I was so much better when I was younger,' she said. 'Who knows, maybe I could've been a half decent pianist if I hadn't been so lazy ... Though no, I didn't have the confidence. Sorry, I don't know why I'm telling you this.'

'I'm Julia Stark and this is Sidney Mendelson, my ... colleague,' said Julia, taking a seat in an armchair.

'Pleased to meet you.'

Siri reached for the ring from the top of the piano and pushed it onto her right middle finger.

'Pretty ring,' said Julia.

'Thank you. It was my mother's.'

Sidney shook Siri's hand, guiding her away from Julia and over to another of the chairs.

'We're a little later than planned, so we haven't had time to change yet, but I thought we might chat now,' said Julia. 'You were at the shareholders' meeting on Sunday?'

'That's right,' said Siri, nervously smoothing her hair.

Her dress was low-cut, emphasising her bony chest.

'Did anything out of the ordinary happen?'

'No, just the usual – the shareholder roster, election of a chair and so on. PG went through the annual accounts, profits, the auditor's response, blah, blah, blah,' Siri explained, her cheeks and throat growing flushed. 'Then we had to approve the accounts, of course, and André suggested disposing of assets, like always... Is that what it's called? I suddenly can't remember. Anyway, that motion didn't pass – big surprise. No one paid any notice to me, Monika looked all tense and strained, Björn pretended to be asleep, and that was about it.'

She rapped the armrest of her chair with her knuckles.

'What do you mean, no one paid any attention to you?'

'I... They never do, but during any other business I brought up the idea of making Mannheim into a conference hotel. I didn't mean immediately, obviously, I just wanted to broach the subject.'

'What did they say about that?' asked Julia.

'Oh, you know. Old money's all that matters, anything else is vulgar, but at the same time ... the forbidden thought of having *more* money is like giving a vampire a whiff of blood.'

'So none of the others liked your idea?'

'PG just said thanks and moved on to the next item on the agenda. I hadn't done enough preparation, I know that; I never do. I kept rambling and apologising, and everyone was probably just thinking: God, what a pain ... A bit like you right now.'

'We appreciate you being honest,' said Sid.

'OK, good,' she said, blushing again.

'How was the dinner that evening?'

'PG drank too much, Björn drank too much ... I'm not judging – it is what it is,' said Siri, wetting her lips. 'Monika was playing hostess, being polite to everyone but me – she was annoyed with me. I mostly kept quiet, paying more attention to my phone. I had a grappa with André in the Red Room afterwards, then I went home before it all got too much.'

'What time was that?'

'Just after ten, I think.'

'Alone?' asked Julia.

'Always alone.'

'You walk from here?'

'Yes.'

'What does Björn do?'

'He can manage to get home if he's not too drunk, but André or I usually go with him. Otherwise PG does it.'

Sid got up and took out his phone. 'We'd like you to take a look at a photograph that—'

'Yes, I've heard.'

'That's quite unpleasant,' Sid tried again.

Siri took the phone from him and studied it with a frown. Her pupils slowly widened, and she used two fingers to enlarge the image, a sudden look of horror on her face.

'It's Werther,' she whispered.

'The man in the picture?'

Her lips were trembling as she looked up at Julia.

'It's Werther,' she repeated.

'Are you sure?'

'The scar on his stomach ... He got it in a forestry accident, I think. It's him.'

Julia looked at the photograph again. The man's shirt had ridden up, baring his large belly, a string of hair between his navel and the waistband of his trousers. The photograph was slightly blurry, and she had assumed it was simply a roll of fat, but she saw now that the fold on his stomach actually sloped a little too sharply for that.

Siri dried her cheeks with the back of her hand. Sid got up to fetch a napkin for her, and she nodded in thanks, her face crumpling again.

'Werther ... I can't believe it. Who could want to hurt him?' she asked, trying to compose herself.

'Someone,' said Julia. 'Clearly.'

# 15

Julia and Sid climbed the broad staircase, turning off into the corridor towards their rooms.

Back in the drawing room, Siri had started weeping. Sid had attempted to comfort her, getting to his feet and wrapping his big arms around her. They made a handsome couple, Siri's pretty face resting against his chest as she slowly composed herself.

Julia had waited for a moment and then said they would give Siri some time while they went to get changed.

She was now walking down the corridor beside Sid, the sconces casting a fragmented glow on the right-hand wall.

'Björn, Siri and André all lack an alibi for the time when the photograph was taken, and PG was actually spotted coming back from the direction of the brewhouse just before twelve,' Julia summed up, taking in the dead flies that had collected in the bottom of a glass lampshade.

'From a purely physical point of view, Björn can't have taken the phone or put it back... and Monika and Amelie were both trying to save the rug, giving each other an alibi,' Sid continued.

'Let's focus on Siri, André and PG for now, though I suspect this is only the beginning.'

'You look sad,' said Sid.

'I'm just having a bad day,' said Julia, gesturing to her chest.

She paused a few metres from her door, and as she met Sid's eye, she tried to force back the usual despair.

'Julia? I'm here, you know,' he said softly, stroking her cheek.

She gasped at his touch, closing her eyes and giving herself over to the electricity pulsing through her, the hot currents where her self found free reign.

Julia had learned to live alone. She was no longer dependent on Sid; she had created a new life for herself. It was the knowledge that the detective agency was doing so well that the time had come for her to hire a partner that was the problem. She had decided to lure him over to her agency. That was her far-from-impossible plan.

Sid didn't know it yet, but they would soon be colleagues. They would spend their working days together.

Unfortunately this plan had also allowed a flicker of hope to enter her heart – despite the fact that she kept telling herself that simply couldn't happen. The hope that she might also be able to win back his love.

Julia knew it was impossible, that she was only torturing herself with these thoughts, but in her mind's eye she saw herself lying naked on the bed in a dark room, Sid holding a flickering candle as he studied her in its soft glow, kissing every inch of her mangled body.

Once they had made love, they would stand naked together. He would walk around her seven times, wrapping her up in his love again. And after he broke the glass beneath his bare foot, they would finally be reconciled.

## I WILL FIND THE KEY

Sid's hand dropped to his side, and Julia lowered her eyes to the floor, gripping the handle of her cane.

'Dinner in half an hour,' she said, turning to her door without another glance at him.

\* \* \*

Safely in her room, Julia took out her purple chiffon cocktail dress and tried to work out which jewellery would go best with it, eventually deciding not to wear any at all.

She went through to the bathroom and used the toilet, scrolling through social media and leaving a trail of likes and hearts in her wake.

Julia tore off a few sheets of toilet roll, wiped, flushed and washed her hands. She then got into the shower and shaved her legs and armpits, sighing at the sting of the deodorant after she dried herself off.

The mirror was fogged up, and she used a hand to wipe the moisture away, leaning in close in search of wrinkles on her face. Having failed to find any, she touched up her make-up, covering her scar and making herself pretty again, then said a quick hello to her mother in the mirror.

'I've let a sense of longing in,' she confessed. 'But it's OK, I can brush it aside whenever I want.'

As she got dressed, she tried to focus on the echo of all the conversations she'd had that day.

When PG showed up at her office, suit crumpled after the long drive, he had wanted to know one thing: whether he was a killer.

Julia thought about Björn: disabled, drunk and bitter. About André, who didn't hesitate to meet her eye, a smile permanently plastered across his face. Siri, with her nerves and her sensitivity. And Monika, with her mocking little mouth and the intelligent glimmer in her eye. It was so clear that her position in the family had been questioned and that she used sarcasm and self-mockery in an attempt to retain her dignity – however much it hurt her.

Five individuals, but the time had finally come for her to see them all together, interacting with one another.

Julia dabbed a few drops of Chanel No. 19 onto her throat and wrists, grabbed her cane and went out into the corridor, to Sidney's door. She was just about to knock when she heard his voice. He was on the phone to someone, and he sounded happy, almost eager, laughing at something. Without a word, Julia moved back over to her own doorway to wait.

# 16

Julia heard the quiet murmur of voices from the drawing room as she and Sidney made their way down the stairs. He looked good, in a smart black suit, a dark grey shirt and the shoes she had bought him before their wedding.

'You look fantastic,' he whispered, briefly squeezing her hand.

The thought of him seeing other women, possibly even starting a family at some point soon, gave Julia a queasy feeling in the pit of her stomach. The realisation that she was just like the Mott family – childless, trapped, broken – raced through her head.

In the opening between the tall double doors, Monika was waiting for them in a sleek navy silk dress. She smiled when she saw them, offering her cheek to Sid, who kissed her twice, then saying something kind about Julia's dress and taking them through to the bar in the old study.

The others were all dutifully in place. Siri was sitting in an armchair, her eyes fixed on one of the windows. She looked like she was trying not to cry. PG was standing by the fireplace with a glass of water in one hand. He had a burgundy silk scarf tied around his neck, and his white hair was slicked to one side. André pushed Björn over from the bar.

'Champagne?' asked Monika.

'You're spoiling us,' said Sid.

Amelie was behind the bar, and she filled a couple of coupé glasses. Monika took one of them and turned to Julia.

'Blanc de Blancs. Pol Roger, cold and crisp – just like my mother.'

'Thank you,' Julia said with a smile.

As she took the glass, Monika's cool fingers happened to brush her skin. Julia shuddered, causing the champagne to slosh over her hand. She took a step back, steadying herself on her cane.

Her ears were roaring, as though she was underwater.

She didn't hear what Sid and Monika were talking about. All she could do was stare at the droplets of champagne that collected on the foot of her glass before dripping to the floor. A sense of repulsion rose up inside her, and she swallowed hard, felt the sweat beading on her forehead and had to stop herself from dropping to her knees and throwing up.

After a few seconds, the anxiety passed and she was able to look around the room and sip her champagne.

'Well, you've met the better half of the family now,' Monika said in a low voice.

'That was a pretty cruel joke, the one about Björn not having stood on his own two feet for the past five years,' Sid pointed out, his brow creased.

'Perhaps I should have told you that he'd had his driving licence revoked instead,' Monika said with an unperturbed smile.

She tapped her glass to get everyone's attention and then moved calmly into the middle of the room.

'You've all met Julia and Sid now. They'll be our guests here while they try to investigate the circumstances surrounding the awful picture on PG's phone,' she said, raising her glass. 'Cheers, everyone. Please take your seats.'

The only person who didn't return the gesture was Siri. She didn't react at all, just continued to stare through the window.

'Sid Vicious!' Björn shouted across the room, raising his glass to Sid.

'Mazel tov,' Sid called back.

Amelie opened the doors to the dining room, and Monika quietly showed everyone to the seats she had picked out for them.

'Time to stuff more food down the geese's necks,' said André. 'Just sit back and open your beak.'

Siri was still sitting by the window, and he went over to get her. Smiling as ever, he led his little sister to the table. She sat down between her brothers with a hand over her mouth.

'You OK, sis?' Björn asked, his voice surprisingly tender.

'She's just a sensitive soul,' Monika replied, unfolding her napkin.

'Stop it,' Siri whispered.

Julia used her salad fork to tap her glass, clearing her throat before she spoke.

'Sid and I are incredibly grateful for the generosity we've been shown here so far. It's not often we're made to feel welcome in this line of work,' she said, waiting for their polite laughter to fade before she went on. 'But wonderful as it is to get to know you all, we're here for one reason, and that's to find out what happened.'

'Good luck with that,' Björn muttered.

'I don't mean to ruin dinner for anyone,' Julia continued, 'but it doesn't feel right to hold off on telling you that Siri has identified the man in the photograph.'

There was now complete silence around the dinner table. Siri's throat and cheeks were blotchy and red, and she began crying, tears dripping onto her plate.

'For God's sake, Siri,' Monika bristled. 'Just tell us who it is.'

'Siri?' said PG.

'It's Werther,' she replied, chin trembling.

Björn knocked over his champagne glass and swore loudly.

For Julia, every single detail in the room seemed to light up, like dew in bright sunlight, and she took a deep breath. It felt as though she was walking slowly down the aisle of a plane, studying the passengers' faces between the swaying plastic oxygen masks.

PG looked genuinely afraid, verging on queasy.

'My brother? Are you sure?' he croaked.

Monika didn't seem to take in what Siri had said at first; she was more annoyed that Siri had stolen her thunder. After a moment, however, she grew concerned.

André had already put two and two together, and Julia's revelation simply confirmed how smart he was. He half closed his eyes.

Standing in the narrow service hallway, Amelie's face was pale, her jaw tight.

Julia tried to register every single reaction during these precious seconds when time was at a standstill, but she didn't have time before Björn swore for a second time.

'Shit,' he groaned, dabbing at his wet lap with the starched linen napkin.

Julia's body grew heavy again, aching. Monika's hands shook as she picked up her water glass and drank.

'I really would have liked to avoid involving the police,' said PG, closing his eyes.

'Fuck the police,' Björn mumbled.

Moving slowly, PG got up and moved over to the window, gazing out at the forest.

'Everyone is, of course, free to contact the police,' Sid explained. 'But I should point out that you're under no obligation to do so. People are only obliged to involve the police during serious, ongoing crimes.'

'And where do they draw the line for *ongoing*?' André asked with a smirk.

'Unclear,' Sid replied.

'As far as we're concerned, full confidentiality still applies,' said Julia. 'And since no one managed to identify Werther earlier – and no body has yet been found – we would prefer to complete our investigation before involving the police.'

'So you think someone in this room did it?' asked André.

'What do you think?' Julia countered.

# 17

Amelie left the room without a word once she had served the first course. She seemed so anxious that her back was hunched.

'Come and sit down, PG,' said Monika.

'Is this where I'm supposed to confess?' he asked once he got back to his seat.

He attempted a smile, but his face was tired and harried.

On each plate was a small fish burger and three well-fried chips on a spiral of dressing.

'Breaded lemon sole, shredded rocket and red cabbage, dill dressing with chopped shallots, capers and cornichons,' Monika said with a blasé smile. 'The money set aside for these dinners is basically an appanage ... We have no choice but to consume it orally.'

'The big sums are all tied up in the company and the property, of course,' said PG.

They began eating in silence, and Amelie reappeared with a bottle of champagne, topping up their glasses before she hurried off again.

As soon as they had finished their starters and the plates and cutlery had been cleared away, Amelie was back with two bottles of Chateau Plince from Pomerol. When she reached PG, he put a hand over his glass and asked for lemonade instead.

'I'd like to ask a question,' said Julia. 'PG, you mentioned that your father lived for Mannheim, more than anyone else.'

'Yes,' he said, fixing his colourless eyes on her.

'Your father was on top of every detail, from the brass hardware on a cellar door to practically every tree in the forest, and yet—'

'That's how we remember him.'

'And yet he parted with – or lost, depending on how you look at it – thirty per cent of the company,' Julia continued.

'Well, ownership remained within the family, but ... Yes, technically you're right.'

'Why?'

'I think he probably just needed to inject some capital into the business.'

'Then there must be documentation from the deal? A contract or something like that?' said Julia.

'Not that I've seen ... And Sundsvall Bank no longer exists.'

'I might be wrong, but I've always seen the transfer in a different light,' said André, a playful smile on his face.

'How so?' asked Julia.

Amelie came in and served the main course in silence, pouring a red wine sauce rich and glossy with melted butter.

'Skinless sausages made from venison and prime rib mixed with finely chopped bacon, onion and mushroom, braised and cooked in a red wine sauce,' said Monika. 'I'd highly recommend a little of our very own mint jelly.'

'Bon appétit,' said PG.

'Amen,' said Björn.

They all began eating again, cutlery clinking quietly on the china, the shadows of Siri's lashes dancing over her cheeks.

'André, would you like to continue what you were saying, about why you thought Sylvester gave your father a thirty per cent stake?' said Julia.

'Right,' he replied, taking a sip of wine. 'Those of us sitting around the table now are the fourth generation. As you know, the man who created this empire was our great grandfather, Mannheim Mott.'

'Cheers to that,' PG spoke up, taking a sip of water.

'But in order to avoid splitting the company, his eldest son – Leopold – inherited everything,' André continued, 'while our grandfather got nothing. Zilch. Pretty unfair, you might think, but it's a classic example of a fideicommissum.'

'Cheers to that,' said Monika.

'But times moved on, and things had already started to go downhill by the time Sylvester took over from Leopold. Our father, Augustus, was allowed to live in the house by the river. He worked as a foreman for the company, but ... and this is when it happens, because Sylvester was an honourable man, in the old-fashioned sense of the word. And he decided to compensate his cousin for the unfair inheritance rules.'

'Our dad might not have got half, but he ended up with thirty per cent,' said Siri.

'I'd still very much like to see any paperwork covering the deal,' said Julia.

'We only have the updated registration documents and the new ownership structure, but it doesn't show what came before,' said André.

'I'll have a look. There might be other documents,' said PG.

They continued their dinner, conversations branching off and moving around the table again. André tried to explain something about renovating furniture to Sid, and Björn laughed sarcastically at him. Monika checked from time to time that PG was still sticking to water. Siri stared down at her plate, her food practically untouched.

The family's attempts to put on a united, warm front had seemed wafer-thin from the very outset. Everyone praised the food – as they no doubt did every time – and Amelie smiled her usual smile as she cleared away their dishes, but ultimately they were incapable of restraining themselves, even though they had guests. It was as though every one of them was convinced they belonged to a natural elite, each with their own specific combination of intelligence, charm and self-deprecation, spirituality, generosity and open-heartedness.

The evening light flooded in through the large windows, transforming the chandelier from a frosty shade of white to shimmering amber. A dusty cobweb swayed back and forth in front of a grille on the ceiling.

Björn leaned back with a groan. Several buttons were missing on his shirt, and Julia could see a sliver of his plastic brace in the gap.

Dessert consisted of vanilla ice cream on a bed of smooth sauce made from white wine, sugar, lemon and avocado. Amelie had balanced the acidity perfectly with the sugar and the creamy avocado, giving it an overwhelming elegance.

Julia raised her spoon to her lips and thought about PG and André's wildly contrasting views on why Augustus had ended up with thirty per cent of Mannheim. The fact that it was either an attempt to inject capital or to dull Sylvester Mott's guilty conscience.

'Cheers to Werther,' PG said with little enthusiasm.

Monika nodded and put a hand on his arm. André raised his glass, and Sid took a sip of whisky, his eyes on the table.

'Yeah, what the hell,' Björn sighed.

He shook the last few drops from his cognac glass into his espresso cup, downed the coffee and then slumped back in his wheelchair.

'Say what you like about my brother,' PG said quietly, 'but for those of you who don't know, Werther was the one who found our mother after she died ... It was a real shock – he was only a child – and it changed him, made him angry and frustrated. I'm not trying to defend him, but he was actually a good brother before that.'

'Well, now you've said it,' Monika mumbled.

'May I ask whether Werther was cremated in the blaze the other night?' asked Björn.

'I spoke to the technicians working on the investigation,' said Sid. 'They haven't found any human remains.'

Siri let out a sob, and Monika shot her an irritated glance. 'Sorry, is it your brother who died?'

Siri stared at her in disbelief. 'I'm just a bit upset and—'

'And you love the attention, we know,' Monika snapped. 'All eyes on you, there's nothing you like more. I see you've chosen something suitably low-cut for—'

'Because I'm a whore, no?' Siri interrupted her, getting up from her chair. 'Maybe you—'

'That's your choice of words, but—'

'Maybe you should try opening your legs every once in a while, save PG some money,' Siri spat out in a shrill voice.

'Careful, my friend.'

'Is that what you tell him?'

Monika leapt up, making her dessert spoon clatter against the plate. She took a step forward and slapped Siri hard across the cheek. Siri's head snapped to one side, and she stumbled briefly before managing to regain her balance.

'I think it's time you went to bed,' said Monika.

Siri clutched her cheek, her entire body shaking. She slowly turned towards Monika and lowered her hand. Her eyes were wide, her cheek red.

'You're pathetic,' she hissed. 'You would protect him even if he—'

'Oh, what do you know about love?'

'Nothing,' Siri replied, turning on her heel.

# 18

PG's white hair was standing on end as he got to his feet, mumbled that dinner was over and left the dining room. André and Björn followed their sister out without a word. Monika's movements were jerky, adrenaline still flooding through her veins as she started to help Amelie clear the table.

Julia and Sidney thanked the two women for dinner and then made their way through to the Red Room. They found PG standing by the bar cart, a full glass of whisky in his hands. He raised it in a toast as they came in.

'What was all that about?' Julia asked.

'It sounded private, don't you think?' PG replied.

Julia suspected that Sid was about to apologise for her lack of sensitivity, but he stopped himself at the last minute.

She took a step forward, leaning heavily on her cane.

'What is Monika covering up for you?' she asked, looking him straight in the eye.

'I'll plead another gap in my memory there.'

PG knocked back his whisky and set down his glass, then mumbled 'good night' and walked away. The parquet floor creaked beneath him.

Sid poured a couple of small grappas, and they sat down in the armchairs. They toasted, sipped and then both got lost in thought about what had just happened in the dining room.

Monika came through to the Red Room, marching straight over to them and putting coasters beneath their glasses. Her dress was now creased on her chest, her neatly made-up face shiny and her eyes tired.

'I'd like to apologise for my behaviour this evening. It was stupid and undignified in every sense,' she said.

'Oh, you don't need to worry about us,' Julia told her.

'It was an incredibly generous dinner,' said Sid.

'We know that our presence here creates tension,' Julia continued. 'Or adds fuel to existing tensions, in any case.'

'Though this was my fault,' said Monika. She seemed genuinely upset. 'I've got a sharp tongue, and I get into arguments a little too often ... which is stupid, really, because I always lose.'

'What happened?' asked Julia.

'Another?' Monika suggested.

'Just a small one,' said Sid, handing her his glass.

Monika went over to the bar cart and topped up his grappa, then poured herself a whisky and came back.

'Thank you,' Sid said as he took the glass.

Monika sat down in an armchair, right on the very edge of the seat. Her back was straight, her knees pressed tightly together.

'I honestly don't know why I'm always making digs at Siri,' she said.

'What do you think?' asked Julia.

'I mean, she's coquettish, but that's not exactly illegal ... She's always taunting me for marrying into the family, too,' said Monika, sipping her whisky. 'She's a little rough around the edges, but that doesn't make her a whore. I don't actually know a thing about her sex life – other than the fact that I once saw the morning after pill in her bag.'

The moon was bright outside, and the mosaic of coloured glass in the leaded windows cast pale patterns onto the wooden floor.

'I wonder if you could shed some light on what Siri was getting at,' Julia tried again. 'What exactly has PG done that you're covering up?'

'I really don't know what she meant,' Monika whispered.

'OK,' said Sid.

'It seemed as though you did,' Julia persisted.

'Well, our sex life, clearly, but she doesn't know anything about it. We have separate bedrooms because he snores like a wood chipper, but that doesn't mean ... you know.'

'What?' Julia asked, fully aware that Sid was now squirming uncomfortably.

'That we don't have a sex life.'

'Do you?' she asked.

'Is that relevant?' Monika attempted a smile.

'It might be.'

'I don't think so.'

'We're trying to put the pieces of a puzzle together here.'

Through the glass doors on the bookshelves, she could see countless leather-bound volumes. The night seemed to have grown darker outside, as though the forest had taken a few steps closer to the manor house.

'We have a sex life,' Monika replied, slowly drinking another mouthful of whisky. 'It used to be better, though it was probably never fantastic. But the important thing is that we love each other, we give each other plenty of tenderness ... And that's enough for me.'

'But not for him,' Julia filled in.

'You're not so keen on physical contact yourself,' Monika snapped.

'No.'

Monika leaned forward and set her glass down on the table. 'I know I have no reason to be embarrassed,' she began, taking a deep breath before she continued. 'But PG does things sometimes ... I've told him he needs to be honest with me, because once we start lying to each other we'll drift apart, there'll be nothing we can have a real conversation about any longer; we'd only be together out of convenience then, and I can't live my life like that. I might seem cold and hard, but I need closeness, feelings, contact, just like anyone else.'

'What sort of things does he do?"

'I don't know that I need to get into the detail, but he drinks a lot, as you know ... And sometimes, well, unfortunate things happen.'

Keeping her face neutral, Julia leaned in to Monika, giving her no room for escape. Sid sipped his grappa, managing a kind, patient expression.

'I've read the contract PG signed with you ... Your duty of confidentiality also extends to me, no?' Monika asked once the silence grew unbearable.

'Of course,' Julia replied.

'This is going to sound much worse than it is,' she began, 'but PG often takes pictures in order to remember what he's done, pictures he shows me before begging for forgiveness ... I know you're going to think that must be what the image of Werther is, but PG isn't violent, he never has been, and I know ... I really do think he tells me the truth, which isn't something every wife can say.'

'So what sort of thing does PG get up to?'

Monika pushed back a lock of red hair with trembling fingers. 'God ... He might show me a picture of three bottles of gin after he promised not to drink, or a line of cocaine on a mirror ... racehorses and old bongs. Pictures from the car, when he's driving under the influence. He crashed into a deer once, I'll never forget that.' Monika's voice was calm and composed, but tears began spilling down her cheeks, dripping into her lap. 'But most ... most of the pictures are of Rosita.'

'Who is that?' asked Julia.

'A prostitute in Sundsvall, which ... I find pretty tough,' Monika continued, her voice now faltering. 'You want to be enough for your husband, you know? He says that's not why, that of course I'm enough, I'm his one true love ... And I accept that, even though I know it's not true. So, yes ... It touched a nerve when Siri said what she said.'

Sid got up and grabbed a few napkins from the bar cart, handing them to Monika without a word before taking his seat again.

'Your husband pays for sex, which is illegal under Swedish law. And you accept that,' said Julia.

'Honestly, though, what's not against the law here?' Monika replied with a smile, dabbing beneath her eyes.

'You don't have to defend him.'

'I know, but—'

'Why do you accept all this?' asked Julia.

'Why? Because we've built a life together. PG isn't perfect, far from it, but where else would I go? I know that he loves me. Clearly I can't provide everything he needs, but I'm still worth a lot.'

She folded the used napkins, setting them down beside her half-full whisky glass. She then got up and smoothed her dress over her hips.

'Well, now you know my dirty little secret ... Good night,' said Monika, turning and walking away.

# 19

Julia and Sid were sitting at one corner of the enormous dining table, eating a hearty breakfast of fried sausage, potato and egg. They finished off with a cup of strong coffee and a slice of pie with homemade cherry compote and vanilla sauce.

Sid was busy replying to various messages on his phone, and Julia had to stop herself from stealing glances at the screen.

She set her cup down on the table and thought about the fact that none of what Monika had told them last night suggested PG was violent. Though on the other hand, a man's relationship with his older brother was governed by entirely different rules than that with his wife.

'What are you thinking?' asked Sid.

'That being a private detective suits you,' she said with a smile.

'Are you kidding?'

'No, I could get used to having you as my colleague,' Julia told him, her heart racing.

She turned her head towards the window, fully aware that this was the moment when she should ask him whether he would ever consider making the leap.

'How long do you think this is going to take?' Sid asked, putting down his cutlery.

'Why, are you angling for a raise?' she replied.

'No, I just need to know. A few things have come up at work.'

'We'll be done soon.'

'But you no longer think André is the killer, do you?'

'I haven't ruled anyone out yet,' she replied. 'But no, I know it was probably a bit rash of me to accuse him … I did it because what surprised him wasn't that Werther was planning to come to the meeting but that it was Björn who told us.'

'Do you know something I don't?'

'No.'

'But you still think you'll be able to solve this soon?'

'I'll be done in two days,' she replied, pronging a few slices of sausage onto her fork.

'You sound sure.'

'Are you doubting me?'

'Never.'

'Want to make a bet?'

'No.' Sid grinned.

'Let's bet dinner. I need two days to find the key.'

'OK, deal.'

'If I win, you take me out to dinner.'

'And if you lose?'

'I won't,' she said.

'Hypothetically.'

'Then you can take your sweet colleague out to dinner instead,' said Julia, getting up from the table.

\* \* \*

An hour later, Julia and Sid made their way down the corridor to PG and Monika's private suite on the ground floor to meet them in the large office.

They paused in front of the open door. Julia used her cane to knock and then stepped inside, Sid following her in onto the worn blue cashmere rug.

There was a diagonal crack in the window, warping the world outside. Fine veils of drizzle hung over the garden, flanked as ever by the tall, dark pines.

PG had come straight from the forest, needles in his hair and pale bark chips clinging to his green fleece sweater. He gestured to the four brown leather armchairs around the low coffee table, where a collection of commemorative medals were on display.

Monika was perched on the edge of the dark desk, drinking an iced latte through a metal straw. She was wearing a pale blue Chanel skirt suit interwoven with silver thread and a pair of low white pumps.

'Can I get either of you a drink?' she asked, switching off the green banker's lamp.

'We're fine, thank you,' Sid replied, taking a seat.

Julia moved over to the window and gazed out at the dense trunks and the dark green needles. She could just imagine the damp scent, the undergrowth, all the mushrooms, seeds and larvae. The trees took nourishment from their predecessors, growing on layer upon layer of death, rising from the rotting, decaying plants.

'You asked for a meeting,' said PG.

Julia shuddered, dragging herself back into the room. She nodded and turned around, lowering her cane to the floor and meeting his eye.

'Monika told us about the photographs you take,' she said.
'What the hell,' he snapped.
'Sorry, but I don't want to keep lying,' Monika said quietly.
'Oh for God's sake,' he sighed, fixing his eyes on her.
'I'm not the one who should be ashamed, PG. I'm really not.'

It was plain to see that he hadn't been expecting this conversation, and wasn't quite in control of his reaction.

'OK, Monika,' he snapped, running his fingers through his hair. 'I'm ashamed of all of this, of course I am ... But these sins of mine, they stop me from digging my own grave quite so quickly and—'

'Stop,' she interrupted him.

'And I'd like to remind you that you don't have to stay married to me if you don't want to.'

'You know I do, but that doesn't mean I don't get upset by the things you do. Because I do. What sort of person would I be if I didn't?'

'Someone who knows me,' he suggested. 'Who accepts me for who I am ... Who understands that I do what I have to in order to cope with my lot.'

'It still upsets me,' she mumbled.

'I'm a weak person, much too weak for this life and ... and if it wasn't for Mannheim and the forests, I just wouldn't be able to do it.'

'I'm here for you,' she said. 'But are you here for me? I can't cope with these lies, I need to know the truth about what happened to Werther ...'

'And so you told them just how awful I am?'

'Monika was simply answering our questions following the argument with Siri yesterday evening,' Julia explained. 'I didn't give her any choice. Her only other option would have been to lie to our faces.'

PG sighed and stroked the arm of his chair. He picked at one of the leather-clad buttons for a moment and then looked up.

'Just so you know,' he said, his voice remarkably composed, 'this is exactly what I hoped to avoid getting into when I contacted you instead of the police.'

'You hired us to get to the bottom of what happened and—'

'I know,' he snapped.

'And our duty of confidentiality will apply even if you decide to terminate the contract,' said Julia.

PG sat quietly, breathing heavily. 'No, keep going . . . even if I am starting to get an idea of where this is headed,' he mumbled.

'Then I'm afraid I need to ask for access to all the photographs on your phone and computer,' Julia explained.

'That feels rather intrusive.'

'We'll need to look at Monika's phone and computer too,' said Sid.

'OK, I'll get them,' she whispered, getting up and leaving the room.

Three hours later, Sid and Julia had gone through all the archived, hidden and deleted images on each device. They hadn't found anything linked to Werther's death, but they did find five deleted photographs on PG's computer, taken on his mobile phone, that confirmed what Monika had told them.

In the first, he had documented his wet trousers and one shoe on a filthy floor. There was an empty vodka bottle by his feet, plus an old betting slip from the racetrack.

The next image showed the broken rear light of a parked car.

The remaining three photographs were all of a slim, dark-haired woman with serious eyes. She looked to be in her forties, and the images showed her sitting topless on a kitchen chair, illuminated from behind as she exhaled cigarette smoke; lying naked on a bed with a line of cocaine stretching from her navel to her crotch, and finally: holding up a used condom and laughing.

'OK, let's check their messages and emails next. Social media and search history too,' said Julia.

'Shall I do Monika's?'

'Whatever you like.'

Julia opened PG's mail platform and scrolled slowly through his messages, read and unread alike. She went back two years in time before switching to his sent folder, drafts, deleted messages and junk mail.

'Sid,' she said, a sudden intensity in her voice.

He left Monika's laptop on the coffee table and moved behind Julia at the desk. Sid read the email that had ended up in PG's spam folder.

*Little brother,*

*My lot in life has never been to do the right thing, but I still take pleasure in just how right it is that the end is nigh for the withering Mott family.*

*Our generation's only merit is that we seem to have had the good sense to remain childless, meaning the question of inheritance can finally be put to bed.*

*I am writing to inform you that I plan to attend the AGM tomorrow in order to use my twenty-five per cent share to vote in favour of selling Mannheim and dividing up the assets once and for all.*

*This information is for your eyes only, and I urge you to delete this email from your devices just as I intend to from mine.*

*Kind regards,*
*W.*

'Hang on ... What the hell is this?' Sid asked in disbelief.

'I know, it's a lot to take in,' Julia replied, looking up at him. 'Werther announced, completely out of the blue, that he was planning to attend the meeting for the first time in years.'

'Just like Björn said ...'

'Which means he must have been in touch with Werther.'

They checked the sender and could only conclude that there was no misunderstanding werther@mott.com.

'So, Werther wanted to sell Mannheim, but he was murdered before he got a chance to vote in favour of it,' says Sid. 'Which means we need to ask who might have been prepared to kill him in order to stop the sale.'

'Or to inherit his share.'

'If he didn't have a will then his brother would inherit everything.'

'The arrow keeps swinging back to PG, doesn't it?' Julia mused.

'But PG is also the only person we can be sure *didn't* know that Werther was coming . . . The email was unread in his junk mail. I mean, if he'd wanted to hide the message surely he would have just deleted it and emptied the trash folder?'

Julia gripped her cane in one hand, placed the other palm on the desk and forced herself up.

'But the strangest thing,' she said, looking up at Sid, 'is that Werther mentions having a twenty-five per cent share, not thirty-five.'

# 20

The Stark Detective Agency set up a temporary office in Sid's room, and they spent the rest of the morning on their phones and computers. Julia couldn't help but think that this was what every day would be like if she managed to win Sid over.

They paused to share information from time to time, to give each other updates and for coffee.

Julia glanced over to Sid, who was sitting with his knees wide apart, scrolling through the information on his screen.

'Classic manspreading,' she said.

'Sorry, but—'

'Women have genitals too, you know.'

'Did you interrupt me just to say that?' he asked, raising an eyebrow.

'Yes ... And that I've been in touch with the Companies Registration Office. The letter about the updated division of shares hasn't gone out yet, but the transfer is complete and registered. Werther signed over ten per cent of Mannheim to Björn two weeks ago.'

'That's a smoking gun if ever I saw one,' said Sid.

'Pretty much.'

'Shit,' he whispered.

'Everything OK?'

'I think I've found Rosita on a couple of escort sites. Her face is hidden, but she calls herself Rosebud, Rosita Rosebud, and she's got a studio in Sundsvall.'

'Reach out to her,' said Julia.

'Really?'

'Book a time with her as soon as possible.'

'OK,' he said with a shrug.

'I've requested PG's prenup from the Tax Authority, but it'll probably be a while before they send it over.'

'We'll keep going in the meantime.'

'OK, I'll start with taxis and trains,' said Julia.

Just thirty minutes later, she had established that Werther had taken a pre-booked cab to the station in Östersund at 10.45 on the morning of the AGM. He boarded the train to Sundsvall at 11.27 and, according to the conductor, got off at 13.53. The CCTV cameras at the station backed this up, capturing a man matching Werther's description at that exact time. He then walked in the direction of the taxi rank, where he got into one of the waiting cars and disappeared out of shot.

'We need to talk to the driver of that cab,' Julia whispered.

Right then, they heard raised voices outside. She and Sid got up from their computers and went over to the window to see what was going on. There was no sign of anyone in the section of yard they could see, and so Sid lifted the latch and opened the window. Monika's panicked voice grew much louder.

'PG!' she shouted. 'PG!'

Julia gripped Sid's arm as they rushed out of the room. The foot of her cane thudded against the carpeted floor in the hallway, the amber glow of sconces flickering by out of the corner of her eye. By the time they reached the staircase, Monika was inside. Her voice was close to breaking as she continued to shout from the drawing room.

'PG!'

They hurried after her, catching up with her as she was on her way back through the dining room. Monika's cheeks were red, and her shoes and tights were muddy.

'What's going on, Monika?'

'Have you seen PG?' she panted.

'No, not since this morning,' said Sid.

'Oh, God ...'

'What's going on?' Julia repeated.

'Werther's body,' Monika replied, on the verge of tears. 'It's in the water ... I think it must be him, anyway. Over by the dam. I need to talk to PG.'

'Are you sure he's dead?' asked Sid.

'You said—'

'But didn't you check whether or not he was alive?' he cut her off.

'I thought ...'

Sid turned and ran towards the main entrance, and Monika slumped down onto a chair. Julia leaned heavily on her cane.

'I didn't think ... I thought ...'

'Don't worry, he's probably dead, but until we know for sure we have to ...'

'Of course, of course, but it looked like ...'

She trailed off, tears spilling down her flushed cheeks.

'What did it look like?' asked Julia.

'This is crazy,' she whispered. 'I don't understand any of this, I—'

'Stay here,' said Julia, hurrying after Sid.

She left the manor house and made her way along the gravel path between several smaller buildings. The air was warm and damp, bees buzzing around the clover and common horsetail.

Julia passed some white garden furniture in a sheltered seating area and continued down a stone staircase until she had a better view.

The old dam was built from huge blocks of granite, and there was a drop of at least ten metres to the glittering brook in the middle of the dry riverbed on the other side. The sluice gate was made from tarred logs, and thin streams of water sprayed out between the cracks. There was a cloud of water vapour hanging in the air, shimmering like a rainbow in the sunlight.

She could see the red wooden chapel in the distance, plus the old mill with its dry blade wheel and the remains of the water-powered saw.

Swallows swooped through the air above the river, hunting insects.

Julia continued around a cluster of trees and spotted Sid standing on the bridge that formed the crest of the dam. He was on his phone.

She gripped the cast-iron railing in order to keep her balance as she approached.

When she realised he was speaking to the police, she paused and turned to the water.

The mirror-flat surface of the lake was almost level with the top of the dam. The man was floating on his back between the water lilies. His swollen face was the colour of wax, the wound on his head dark against his pale skin.

# 21

An hour later, the authorities had cordoned off the area around the dam with blue and white tape. There were four emergency vehicles on the gravel track, and the paramedics were busy unloading a gurney from the back of the van. The forensic technicians documented the scene and took samples from the dead man.

Sidney was chatting to two officers from the Sundsvall Police, but he moved off to one side when his phone rang.

The case was now officially a murder investigation.

The forensic technicians had pulled Werther's substantial body out of the water, and he was now lying on a white sheet on the shore, flies buzzing around him. His face looked spongy and swollen, his brown teeth visible in his gaping mouth. His shirt had come open, and there were scraps of vegetation clinging to his hairy chest, the curved scar emphasised by his swollen belly. He was barefoot, his trousers clinging to his legs. His arms were by his sides, his palms upturned, and there were dark bruises around his wrists.

So, this was Werther.

The terrible recluse.

There would be a preliminary investigation into his death. His body would be taken to the nearest forensic department for a post-mortem, and the police would hold interviews with his family in the coming days.

Monika was standing quietly by the cordon, her face pale, staring down at her dead brother-in-law. She had draped a thin down jacket around her shoulders, and her red hair was blowing across her face.

PG's Land Rover pulled up behind the emergency vehicles. He leapt out and ran over to Monika, pulling her to him and forcing her to look away. He held her tight and stroked her back.

Julia studied Werther's dead body as the technicians placed evidence bags over his hands. Her mind drifted as she pictured him on the train, impatiently getting up from his seat the minute the conductor announced that they would soon be arriving in Sundsvall. She imagined him buttoning his jacket, grabbing his bag and moving out into the aisle. The train came to a halt with a slight jolt, and he stumbled forward and regained his balance by gripping the back of a seat.

The doors opened with a hiss, and Werther stepped down onto the platform with a handful of others. His thoughts had probably been on the upcoming meeting, when the decision would be made to divest the group and dispose of property that had been passed down for generations.

He hadn't known that the email he sent PG had never reached its intended recipient, but he clearly wasn't expecting anyone to come and pick him up, because he marched straight over to the taxi rank and got into the first available car.

According to the taxi firm, the driver had taken him to Mannheim, but rather than dropping him off outside the main building, he had asked to get out by the brewhouse. Werther had then paid, left the car and walked off to meet his killer.

He had followed someone into that building – either under duress or oblivious to the threat – and was then bound and killed. His body was subsequently photographed and dumped in the lake.

Julia and Sid's arrival had unnerved the killer, and he or she had set fire to the crime scene in an attempt to destroy any possible evidence.

\* \* \*

It was as though the discovery of Werther's body had knocked the wind out of everyone. PG and Monika both seemed lost and absent. The lunch they had planned was cancelled, and they announced that anyone who wanted to was welcome to join them for a sandwich in the kitchen instead – 'Like a Dutchman,' PG mumbled.

His face was ashen – he had just lost his brother, after all – and he looked at Julia and Sid as though he could no longer remember why they were there.

Amelie clearly didn't want anyone to go hungry. She had made long open sandwiches for everyone, slicing the white bread lengthways and arranging eight different toppings on top: prawn salad; gravlax; soused herring; cheese, tomato and lettuce; sliced egg; smoked ham; meatballs, and roast beef with remoulade.

Julia found herself wondering what impact it had on a person to have someone like Amelie constantly on hand, ever-present like some sort of shadow. Someone who made their beds and cleaned the house, did the washing and cooked all their food without ever really being thought of as part of the family.

PG, Monika, Sid and Julia each cracked open a bottle of beer and sat down on the stools around the kitchen island. They had just started eating when André appeared in the doorway.

'Siri told me the news, PG ... I'm so sorry.'

PG nodded, and Monika's face crumpled as though she was about to start crying, though she quickly composed herself.

'Do you want a sandwich?' PG asked, his voice hoarse.

'Please,' said André, taking a seat. 'Though I can't stay long. Björn fell asleep on the way over here. I left him in the shade ... didn't have the heart to wake him.'

PG cleared his throat. 'The funeral will be tomorrow, in the chapel.'

'The post-mortem might not necessarily be finished by then,' Sid hesitantly spoke up.

PG simply waved his hand, explaining with no real conviction that they couldn't stop him from holding a memorial for his brother.

'Maybe I'm missing something, but shouldn't Tweedle Dum and Tweedle Dee here be heading home now?' asked André. 'Or what's happening?'

Julia straightened up. 'Now that Werther's body has been found,' she said, 'the police will want to talk to you all. And as soon as they have a suspect, the prosecutor will take over the preliminary investigation.'

'What should we do?' Monika asked. She seemed anxious.

'Do?' PG repeated. 'I'm going to show them the picture, be honest with them. I'll tell them everything I've told you.'

'Fine, but they'll throw you in a cell in Saltvik,' said Monika.

'Is that true?' he asked, turning to Julia.

'I honestly don't know.'

'Maybe we should just find you a good lawyer,' Monika suggested.

'Stop,' said PG.

'Don't do anything stupid now,' she mumbled.

'Am *I* stupid?' PG asked the others.

'I've always viewed your desire to get to the bottom of what happened as genuine,' said Julia.

'I need answers,' he confirmed.

'And we can help with that,' said Julia. 'I can't promise they'll be the answers you're hoping for, but you'll find out the truth if you—'

'Seriously, sweetie,' André interrupted her with a smile. 'PG, you know it's her job to say all this stuff, don't you? They want your money. They don't give a damn about the fucking truth.'

'Don't be so rude,' Monika snapped.

'At least the police won't send you an invoice for locking you up.'

'I need two days to solve the puzzle,' said Julia, feeling her face grow hot.

'That's what we think, what we're hoping,' Sid hurried to add.

'Can I have that? Will you give me two days?' she asked, meeting PG's eye.

'OK,' he nodded.

\* \* \*

Once they had finished eating, Sid and Julia followed André out onto the gravel in front of the manor. Björn was still fast asleep in his wheelchair at the foot of the stairs.

'What did he look like? Werther, I mean,' André asked, lighting a cigarette.

'He'd been in the water for nearly a week,' said Sid.

'In terms of injuries, though. He hadn't been chopped up or anything?' As ever, he smiled.

'We'll have to see what the pathologist says,' Julia replied, giving Sid a discreet nod.

A few twittering birds lifted off from the edge of the fountain, and the sharp smell of pine drifted in on the wind.

Sid placed a heavy hand on André's shoulder, making it slump under the weight, and he looked him straight in the eye.

'We know that Werther transferred ten per cent's worth of shares to Björn,' he said.

'That's true,' André replied, taking a step back.

'Neither of you mentioned this when we were talking about the percentages at dinner yesterday,' said Sid.

'The transfer was complete, but it hasn't been registered properly yet ... We didn't want an argument, so we thought it'd be better to wait until everything was done. That's the usual approach,' André explained.

'We'd like to see the paperwork surrounding the deal,' said Julia.

'There was no deal. Werther just gave Björn ten per cent,' he grinned.

'Why? Why would he give him ten per cent of the company?'

'Because Werther had a heart of gold ... or some other metal,' André replied, looking down at his cigarette. 'He put my brother in a wheelchair and promised to compensate him for that, but he spent years prevaricating – until I said I'd get a lawyer if we didn't agree on something soon.'

'Ten per cent of the company seems like a pretty high level of compensation,' Sid pointed out.

'Sure, but it wasn't a case of him trying to do the right thing, it never has been,' said André. 'He paid up because he didn't want the family name dragged through the mud.'

Björn woke up with a cough, exhaling wearily. 'What's going on?' he asked, looking up at them.

'We're heading home,' said André.

'Aw, did I miss the whole shindig? Any good grub?'

'Sandwiches and lager.'

'Lager,' he muttered.

'Björn, I saw you out here early on Wednesday morning, heading in the direction of the brewhouse,' said Julia.

'I live here.'

'You live almost four kilometres away.'

'I might not have been totally sober, but—'

'You don't have to tell them,' André butted in.

'But I realised I was out of booze, and I had the great idea to come over here at one in the morning to bang on the door and borrow a few bottles ... Only, I changed my mind.'

'What made you change your mind?' asked Julia.

'I didn't realise PG and Monika had guests. I saw a woman with her tits out in one of the windows upstairs, and since I didn't feel like much of a Romeo, I gave up.'

'Did you see anything on your way back?' Julia pressed him.

'Nope ... Other than a grey figure down by the brewhouse.' He pointed up towards Mannheim and whispered, '"O, horrible! O, horrible! most horrible!"'

'You like your Shakespeare.' Julia smiled.

Björn responded by pushing the joystick on his wheelchair, swinging sharply and rolling off across the gravel with his safety belt clinking against the spokes.

# 22

Sid and Julia drove across the long Sundsvall Bridge, over the glittering bay that seemed to have been almost hacked into the heart of the city. They took the slip road once they reached the south side and continued onto the E14.

'Tell me about your sweet colleague,' said Julia.

'No.'

'Does she have kids?'

'Two girls.'

Julia swallowed and stared out of the window. The car's satnav took them into a social housing area on the edge of an industrial estate by the motorway.

'How long have you booked with her?' she asked once she was confident her voice would hold.

'An hour's "girlfriend experience",' Sid replied, drumming the wheel.

'What does that involve?'

'No idea, it just sounded the least complicated.'

'OK.'

Julia imagined a bare-faced Rosita in a pair of faded sweatpants and a white vest top, no bra. Setting the washing machine running before she took a John through to her bedroom, lit a candle and said she had been waiting for this all day.

'I've been thinking about PG again,' Sid said after a moment or two. 'Judging by the pictures on his phone, there seems to be some sense of trust between him and Rosita ... Or that's the impression I got, anyway.'

'I know,' said Julia. 'That occurred to me too. But at the same time, it's hard to ignore the imbalance, in terms of power ... It's enormous, in almost every sense: a rich white CIS man with a sky-high socioeconomic status.'

'Et cetera, et cetera,' Sid sighed.

She nodded and thought about the fact that those who buy sex are almost always physically stronger than the person they are buying it from, that the threat of violence is ever-present.

'Someone once said it's the power difference itself that's being sexualised,' she said.

Sid parked the car and they got out, cutting across a scrap of grass to a door with a scratched window.

He entered the door code and held it open for Julia. The stairwell smelled like rubbish and cooking, and the lift was almost entirely covered in graffiti, with black, yellow and gold scribbles all over the walls, mirror and door. There was so much paint on the ceiling light that it put out virtually no light.

Sid's face seemed tense, and Julia could see that he found the situation uncomfortable.

'I know this might seem crazy, but whether Rosita knows anything or not, she's actually our most important character witness – she, if anyone, must know whether PG gets angry or violent,' said Julia.

They got out on the seventh floor, and Sid went over and rang the buzzer on the door marked Olsson while Julia hung back out of view.

She heard a clicking sound as someone uncovered the peephole inside, and then the door opened on the chain.

'Yeah?' said a woman's voice.

'I've got an appointment,' he said.

'What's your name?'

'Sid.'

There was a brief silence, and Julia guessed that the woman was sizing him up before she next spoke.

'Come in, Sid.'

She closed the door to unhitch the chain, then stepped to one side to make room for him.

From where she was standing, Julia saw Sid pause on the threshold, preventing the door from closing.

'I booked an hour with you, and I'll pay for that, but I actually just want to talk to you,' he said.

'OK ...'

'I need to ask you a few questions about one of your clients.'

'Nope, no can do.'

'I'm here with my colleague, Julia. We're private detectives, and we've been hired by Per Günter Mott.'

Julia stepped forward and moved over behind Sid.

Rosita was in her forties, wearing a thick Icelandic sweater, a pair of acid wash jeans and white socks. Her curly hair was tied up in a ponytail, and she studied them with a guarded look on her face.

The ceiling light cast a soft glow over the coat rack and a small chest of drawers with a stack of bills on top. The linoleum on the floor was dark, made to look like slate.

'What the hell is this?' she asked, staring at them.

'We just need to ask you a few questions,' said Julia.

'I don't want to hear it, not my problem.'

'We only want to ask about PG. Not you, not anyone else.'

'Makes no difference, don't you get it?'

'I can call him if you want to make sure we're telling the truth.'

Rosita's right hand was hidden behind her hip, and Julia could see a Burberry bag on the floor beside her.

'You can put the pepper spray back in your bag,' said Sid.

Rosita smirked irritably. Other than blusher and pale pink lipstick, she didn't seem to be wearing any make-up.

'I'd like you to leave now,' she said, raising her voice. 'Just go, leave me alone.'

'We'll go once you've—'

'NOW!'

Rosita held up the little bottle of pepper spray.

Julia took a step forward, leaning against her cane. She looked Rosita straight in the eye, waiting until the woman lowered the bottle.

'Buying sex is against the law in Sweden, but that's not why we're here. We have a duty of confidentiality to PG, meaning we can't report it – but you can, either now or later, if you choose to.'

'What's that got to do with you?'

'Look, my leg is hurting and I'd really appreciate it if I could sit down, just while I ask my questions,' said Julia. She could see that Rosita was wavering. 'I have to ask them; it's my job. But you don't have to answer if you don't want to.'

'Maybe I won't. Maybe I won't say a thing,' she said, lowering her gaze.

'So can we come in?' Sid asked softly.

'You've got forty-five minutes left.'

# 23

SID AND JULIA FOLLOWED ROSITA through to the living room, where a couple of puffy pale leather sofas jostled for space with a black coffee table with candles on top. There was a framed photograph of Rosita on the wall, sitting beside a man in glasses with a young boy on his lap.

Through the bedroom doorway, Julia could see a large black leather headboard. There was a TV mounted on the wall, plugged in to a DVD player on a low bench below.

Rosita showed them into the kitchen, which had a bumpy laminate floor, a rustic pine dining table and three chairs.

'Sit if you need to sit,' she said as she filled the kettle.

'Thanks.'

Julia's cane made a metallic clang as she leaned it against the radiator, and she took a seat and stretched her leg with an over-the-top sigh. Sid moved over to the window and looked out at the empty playground.

'How long has PG been coming to see you?' Julia asked.

'I don't know, maybe seven or eight years,' she said, setting out three mugs and a box of teabags. 'Why don't you ask him this stuff yourself?'

'We will.'

'Roughly how often does he come here?' asked Sid.

'It varies ...'

'On average?'

Rosita opened the fridge and took out a carton of lactose-free milk. 'Sometimes it's once a month and sometimes it's half a year before I see him again ... And then there are times when he comes every single week, or several days in a row.'

'It doesn't sound like he books very far in advance?'

'Nope. He just gives me a call, which is fine by me. I trust him.'

Rosita switched off the kettle, carried it over to the table and sat down.

'His wife Monika knows he comes here,' said Julia.

'I know.'

Sid filled three cups with water, and everyone picked a teabag and dropped it in.

'Does he ever talk about her?' asked Julia.

'Yes.'

Rosita's cheeks were flushed, and she peeled off her sweater and draped it over the back of the chair. Her bare arms were pale and slim, and the thin black vest she was wearing made her seem like a young woman.

'Does he ever mention his brother Werther?' asked Sid.

'Sometimes.'

'What has he told you about him?'

She shrugged. 'I don't know. That he's a recluse, that he used to act like a pig when they were kids ... Nothing special.'

'Would you say that PG hates him?' Julia probed further.

'No ... I mean, I don't know. They obviously had a rough childhood; their mother killed herself.'

Rosita was quiet for a moment, and Julia noticed that the hair on her arms was standing on end.

'Has PG ever showed you any strange pictures?' asked Sid.

Rosita frowned.

'Strange how?'

'Unsettling,' said Julia.

'No, he hasn't. What pictures are you talking about?'

Neither answered her question.

'Has PG ever been violent towards you?' Julia asked instead.

'Look, what is this?' A troubled smile had appeared on Rosita's face.

Julia felt the heat from her teacup making her fingers damp, the air slowly being forced out of her lungs. She saw the sun shining in through the filthy windows, catching every fleck of dust in the air. It illuminated a strand of curly hair on the floor, the greasy fingerprints around the handle on the fridge door.

Time ground to a halt, and everything became weightless.

Julia fixed her eyes on Rosita.

She had dyed her hair recently, leaving a slight shadow around her hairline.

Faded bruises revealed that someone had gripped her upper arms.

The woman wasn't trying to hide anything.

A slight scar by her left eye seemed to blush slightly.

'Has he?' Julia heard herself ask again.

'Towards me? No, he'd never. He's just sad.'

Rosita's face mirrored her memories of PG, and Julia could see his downturned mouth and furrowed brow in her expression.

The slanting light highlighted her pulse in her throat.

Her heart rate slowed slightly.

Rosita was telling the truth.

Julia slumped back in her chair, and the second hand of her wristwatch began ticking again, returning to its usual speed.

'Why is he sad?' asked Sid.

'Why? He just is,' Rosita replied, scratching her neck.

Julia sipped her tea. She could hear a TV in the apartment next door. A children's programme, by the sounds of it.

'I'd like to know ... what exactly does he book when he comes to see you?'

'We never decide in advance. Often he doesn't want anything. We just spend time together, enjoy a glass of wine, chat ...'

'He comes here just to talk to you?'

A flicker of weariness washed over Rosita's face. 'I don't know whether you know, but he's bipolar ... When he's in a manic phase he might want sex, but most of the time he's just really depressed. He cries and cries. And on days like that, all we do is lie in bed together. I listen to him, hold him, tell him that it's all going to be OK.'

# 24

THE ROAD RAN PARALLEL TO the railway, and they had just passed Timrå when they met a seven hundred metre-long train loaded with timber. For the short time that they were driving alongside it, Julia felt as though they were travelling at twice the speed.

'You did well back there,' she said, glancing over to Sid from the passenger seat.

'Thanks, boss.'

'It wasn't the easiest situation. We had no legal grounds to barge in there and interrogate her.'

'I tried to act like a regular cop knocking on her door, so she'd think she had no choice but to let us in.'

'What did you make of her?'

'Not sure. As ever, we'll just have to try to collect all the sparks that were left behind.'

'That's pretty cryptic.' Julia smiled.

'Like a picture, I mean – all the lingering details, her words, her tone.'

'Oh, right, now I understand,' she teased.

'A few sparks were all that was left after the tzimtzum ... when God took a step back in order to make room for the world.'

'Tzimtzum? Is that Jewish dim sum?'
'Seriously?' he said, giving her a disapproving look.
'Sorry, that was stupid. I just wanted to make you laugh.'
'I'm laughing inside,' he said drily.
'I quite like the idea of collecting sparks.'
They left the E4 and continued into the hall of dark pines flanking either side of the road.
'PG must be incredibly lonely if he has to pay someone just to drink a glass of wine with him,' said Sid.
'I don't think we should give too much weight to that side of it, this idea that he goes to her to talk,' said Julia.
'No?'
'No, I think he's a regular John. He goes there for sex and to snort cocaine, it's just that sometimes he's too sad for either.'
'What about her?'
'She wants to feel like they have a special relationship, because that normalises her lifestyle, to an extent.'
'I guess you're right.'
'So, what did you notice? With your cop senses?' asked Julia.
'Not much. She's not a junkie, doesn't have hepatitis, lives alone. Works there too, but she also has a partner and kid – or did have, anyway.'
'Yes, I saw the picture on the wall, but—'
'There was food in the fridge, and the mail on the chest of drawers in the hallway was addressed to Rosita Navarro c/o Olsson.'
'Anything else?'
'She had bruises on her arms.'
'I saw.'

'About a week old,' said Sid.

'But she was telling the truth when she said that PG isn't violent towards her. She didn't feel the urge to hide the bruises when I asked her about that.'

More logging sites raced by outside, the gaping holes left by the forestry machines now overgrown with bilberry bushes and brush.

They passed timber roads behind locked gates, and the tyres crunched as they drove over an area of spilled woodchip.

'I guess there must be a pimp in the picture somewhere,' said Sid.

'Maybe,' Julia mumbled as she opened an email on her phone. 'Hold on ... I've just had a reply from the Tax Authority.'

'Monika and PG's prenup?'

'Bingo,' she said, still reading. 'OK, it says ... Per Günter Mott, blah blah blah ... Ah, here we are: Shares in the company and ownership of the manor house remain separate property and shall be exempted from any settlement in the event of divorce or death.'

'So that's why she's still with him,' Sid muttered.

'Monika doesn't get anything if they split up or if he dies.'

'Poor woman.'

A brief clearing gave way to more dense forest, and the car grew dark again. Julia stole a glance at Sid's profile, at his hands on the wheel and his short, neat hair.

'Why exactly did you book the "girlfriend experience"?' she asked.

'What?'

'Was it a message to me?' she continued with a wry smile.

'What do you mean?' Sid asked, his eyes still on the road.

'That you're trying to say you want to play that sort of game with me.'

'You know the ban on sexual harassment applies to any areas where anti-discrimination laws also apply, right?'

'Are you kidding?'

'I agreed to work for you because I thought you could use my skills,' he replied, his voice neutral.

'Of course,' Julia whispered, gritting her teeth.

'Sorry, I just want to make sure we're on the same page. I don't want you thinking we're getting back together or anything.'

'You could at least let me enjoy the fantasy for a while.'

'That's what I spent seven years doing.'

She knew she had used up every last ounce of goodwill, but she just couldn't help herself. There were times when her longing for him hit with such force that it almost felt like she couldn't breathe. Spending time with him again, sitting beside him in the car, it brought back all the memories, almost as though the past was now.

Julia felt her wedding dress rustle against her ankles as she walked towards the canopy where Sidney and Rabbi Meyer were waiting for her, wrapping Sid up in their marriage by walking around him seven times. Other than the sound of her footsteps and the light movement of her dress, the room had been silent. Nothing had yet happened, everything could still be saved, their marriage was still fresh and promising.

'Sheva Brachot,' she whispered.

'What was that?'

Julia flinched and the memory faded like smoke in the wind.

Outside the car, the trees were still racing by. They were getting close to the gates outside Mannheim. The afternoon light was bright and grey, like a breeze full of ash.

A police car was parked by the side of the burnt-out building, and the entire dam was now cordoned off with blue and white tape.

'You've got two days left if you want to win the bet,' said Sid, glancing over to Julia.

# 25

Julia's alarm clock went off at four the next morning, and she woke feeling so anxious that her heart was racing. She had dreamed that her mother was trying to tell her something with five boarding passes clamped between her lips.

Julia pressed both hands to her face and tried to bring her ragged breathing under control, calming herself by visualising the imaginary photograph from the funeral. Taken from above, she saw a girl in a dark grey dress on the front row of pews. She saw the worn slab floor, all the old ledger stones and wreaths tied with silk ribbon.

Her legs were still shaking ten minutes later when she got out of bed and staggered through to the bathroom to wash her face.

At a quarter to five, she and Sid were in the car with PG and Monika. They had arranged to meet the others in a clearing in the woods to celebrate Foresters' Day. PG had explained that it was tradition in Hälsingland, Medelpad, Jämtland and Ångermanland, with roots stretching back centuries. The family had celebrated Foresters' Day every single year, regardless of wars, stock market crashes and pandemics, suicides, scandals and conflict.

Werther's death wouldn't change that.

The two branches of the Mott family gathered around the fire in the middle of the rounded glade. Veils of mist hung between the trees, and Julia heard a cuckoo crying to the south. PG was wearing a grey jacket and a blue cravat, and he hacked off a fir branch and shook off any water and seeds before returning to the others.

The wind changed direction, and they all moved away from the fire, coughing and spluttering. André was behind Björn, helping to push him across the uneven ground, and Siri bent down to remove a twig that had caught in his spokes. Her nose looked red and sore from crying.

The bottles clinked in the bag Sid had offered to carry, and Monika lowered the picnic basket to a log by the fire. She was wearing a dark brown suit with a mid-length skirt, and she had a mocha coloured headscarf tied around her hair.

'Did you know that spruces can live to an incredible age?' said PG. 'These trees . . . they might just be a couple of hundred years old, but up in the mountains they've found spruces that are ten thousand years old.'

'No way.' Julia was sceptical.

'Not as trees the whole time, of course, they were creeping bushes at some stage . . . but still the same organism, the same genetic individual.'

'Amazing.'

'Foresters' Day is all about thanking and showing respect to the forest. It was here long before us, and it'll be here long after we're gone,' André explained.

## I WILL FIND THE KEY

'Shall we get started?' asked Siri.

'It's meant to be blood, but we prefer booze,' said Monika.

PG pulled a bottle from one of the bags. He poured the brännvin onto the fir branch and started moving around the glade, shaking the alcohol onto the surrounding trees as he thanked the forest.

By the time he returned to the others with the half-empty bottle, his face was slick with sweat. He poured the remainder into seven tapered glasses, and they toasted to the forest and drank in silence.

It was clear to Julia that everyone was unsettled by the situation, but they were still following protocol, as though they had no free will.

It felt like the forest had surrounded them, forcing them together. Bears and wolves circled in the dark wilderness around the brightly-lit glade.

Julia missed her office in Stockholm, her quiet routines. But, she reminded herself, she was going to solve the case within the next twenty-four hours, and then she would be heading home.

The fire crackled, flakes of ash swirling upwards in the dove grey smoke. From a tree nearby, a woodpecker hammered frantically.

Monika unpacked sausages, mustard, cheese sandwiches and beers. PG carved seven long skewers from willow branches and handed them out.

Björn was telling Siri about a Baroque mirror he was busy restoring, with plump-cheeked cherubs made from walnut on the frame.

'I've been thinking about keeping it for myself,' he said with a grin. 'Might be nice to have some cute little angels hovering around the old mug whenever I comb my hair.'

Siri laughed, and for a few seconds Julia saw just how beautiful she was when her face wasn't weighed down with grief.

Swarms of black flies pulsed through the hot air around the fire.

Julia and Sid grilled their sausages above the eager flames. Once the surface was charred and splitting, they moved back with flushed faces and stinging eyes. Everyone ate straight from the skewer, adding a thick squeeze of mustard.

Julia tossed her skewer into the fire once she was done, wiped her hands on a napkin and went to grab a couple of beers for herself and Sid.

'I've just had confirmation of the time of death from forensics,' he told her once she got back.

'Finally,' she muttered.

'Werther died at three in the afternoon.'

'And they're sure?' she asked, taking a swig of beer.

'On the basis of his injuries – a severe blow to the head with some sort of blunt object – and the temperature of his body, the air and water, they say the margin of error is less than ten minutes.'

'So Werther was killed nine hours before the photograph was taken.'

Since the entire family was gathered in the glade, Julia decided to ask them their whereabouts right away. Leaning heavily on her cane, still clutching her bottle of beer, she made her way over to André. He was wearing a sports jacket with a gold monogram on the left chest pocket, and had sat down on a tree stump to eat his charred sausage.

'Tastes better than anything you'd get in a Michelin star joint,' he said cheerily.

'Better setting, too,' she replied, taking another sip of beer.

'And here was me thinking you were a city girl.'

Standing beside him, Julia saw Sid and Siri chatting on the other side of the fire.

'Where were you at three o'clock on the afternoon of the shareholders' meeting?' she asked, turning to André.

'I open the shop for important customers on Sunday afternoons,' he said with a smile.

'Can anyone confirm that?'

'I had a meeting with one of my regulars.'

'Would you mind giving me this customer's name and number?' Julia asked, setting her beer down and taking out her phone to make a note of it.

'Sure ... As soon as you show me some police ID.'

'We can arrange that.'

'Sorry, I don't have anything to hide.' André laughed. 'I just want to respect my clients' privacy.'

'Your girlfriend said you were at her place at that time.'

'Right, we had a coffee.'

'How long did you stay?'

'An hour, maybe?'

'So you closed your shop to these important customers to spend an hour drinking coffee?' Julia summarised.

André shrugged and continued eating. Julia gripped her cane and walked away. The wind had swung around again, and she saw Sid and Siri moving back from the fire. Siri lost her balance, and he caught her. She laughed, her cheeks flushed, her hand lingering on the back of his neck for a moment too long.

Julia made her way over to Björn, who was sitting in his wheelchair at the edge of the glade closest to the forest road. The canvas bag of beer and brännvin was on the ground by his feet, and there were two empty bottles and a glass in his lap. Julia reached for another beer, opened it and handed it to him, asking the same question she had just put to his brother.

'I had a nap after lunch,' he replied, taking a deep swig from the bottle.

'At three o'clock? That's a pretty late lunch.'

'Yup.' Björn stifled a burp.

'Is there anyone who can confirm that?'

'André,' said Björn, draining the last few drops of his beer.

'He says he was with a customer.'

'I have no idea, I was asleep,' he said without looking up at her.

Julia opened another bottle and passed it to him, taking the empties from his lap and putting them down beside the bag.

There was a loud pop as the resin in one of the branches expanded in the heat, sending a shower of sparks several metres into the air.

'There's something I've been wondering,' said Julia. 'When you saw the photograph of Werther's body, you immediately assumed he had been beaten to death.'

Björn shrugged. 'So? Was I wrong?'

'No, you were right – we've just had confirmation of that,' Julia replied. 'But that wasn't something you could have known from the image. He could just as easily have been shot, hanged, stabbed—'

'OK, I get it,' Björn interrupted her.

'Care to elaborate?'

'What?'

'What is it you get?'

'That you think it's damning that I guessed right,' he replied, knocking on the plastic brace beneath his shirt.

'What do you make of that?'

He turned his head and looked up at her with a bitter smile. 'What do I make of it?'

'Yes.'

'That I felt like beating that bastard to death plenty of times ... but I never considered shooting or hanging him.'

# 26

Julia made her way around the fire to join PG and Sid, who were busy grilling more sausages. The smoke made Sid blink, and he asked whether she wanted another. She shook her head and took a step back.

'I'd very much like an interim report,' said PG. 'To hear what you've concluded so far, I mean.'

'It doesn't work like that.'

'What exactly is going on here? I've seen you talking to everyone.'

'We've just found out that Werther died at three o'clock on the day of the shareholders' meeting.'

'I thought it happened in the middle of the night?' PG replied, fixing his bloodshot eyes on her.

'That was when the photograph was taken, yes. Almost nine hours later.'

'Sorry, of course the two could be separate.'

'Where were you at three that afternoon?'

The flames seemed to freeze like shards of glass, ranging in colour from pale blue to deep yellow. Julia turned to PG and saw the warm glow of the fire on his face, that beads of sweat had begun to glisten on his forehead and that he had missed a few white strands on his throat while shaving that morning.

'At three? That must have been around the time Monika was talking to Siri and I was ...' He paused to think, his forehead creased in a forced frown. 'Right, I was in the forest. I went out to site eighteen to calculate the extra time needed because of the rough terrain.'

'Can anyone confirm that?'

'It's lonely in the woods,' he said. As he spoke, the fire began to crackle and twist again.

Time occasionally ground to a halt for Julia, the way it does during an accident, each thousandth of a second etching itself into her memory. It was part of her PTSD, but it also helped her to read faces and subtexts, to see details she otherwise would have missed.

She felt her face grow hot, and she turned away from the fire and went over to Monika, who was sitting on a dark blue blanket on a tree trunk. Julia asked her the same question she had asked the others.

'Siri and I were out on the lake ...'

'At exactly three o'clock?'

'No, we ... We met at two, headed out at around quarter, twenty past. We had coffee and buns, a bit of a picnic in the boat ... Chatted.'

'How long?'

'We didn't get back until half four. We rowed up the river, planned to go all the way to Siri's house and then drive back, but we got into a bit of an argument. That's why it took longer than anticipated.'

'What were you arguing about?'

Monika sighed and folded her arms. 'The usual. Ownership, the patriarchal structure of the company, old injustices – you said, I said, blah, blah, blah ...'

'Think back. The two of you were out on the lake when the murder took place.'

'I just can't believe it ...'

'Did you see or hear anything? Any cars, voices, anything at all ...'

'No, I ... We were so preoccupied, it was so tense. I mean, I'd asked her out onto the lake because I thought we needed it, but I ... You know ...'

'Think back,' Julia repeated.

'I'll try to go over everything in my head once we get home.'

'Thank you.'

Julia began to move away, but she changed her mind and turned back to Monika, leaning on her cane. She felt it sinking into the soft earth.

'Would you mind me asking one more question? I've noticed you share a lot of truths in the form of sarcastic remarks—'

'I'm just trying to get through. I suppose it's a kind of gallows humour.'

'During our first dinner, you joked about Werther's warmth and engagement during the shareholders' meetings.'

'Gosh, I really am awful.' Monika gave Julia an apologetic smile.

'You also said something about him helping PG to smarten up last time he attended,' Julia continued unperturbed.

'Possibly ...'

'I saw that this was something that upset PG.'

'That's because he's always trying to forget or downplay Werther's aggression.'

'And that's why you wanted to remind him of something ... unpleasant?'

Monika took a deep breath, pressed her fingers to her temples and closed her eyes. 'It wasn't a big deal,' she said after a moment. 'It was just so typical of Werther. He was unhappy with PG for one reason or another, and before we knew it he'd marched over and kicked him on the backside – right in front of everyone.'

'Hard to believe that PG could have forgotten that.'

'I know, I was being unkind.'

'Yes, you were,' said Julia, turning and walking away across the glade.

Siri was fiddling with her phone at the far side, and Julia went over to her. A twig broke underfoot.

'Hi, Siri. Where were you at three o'clock on the afternoon of the AGM?' Julia asked, getting straight to the point.

'At three? I do actually know that ... Monika and I were in PG's little rowing boat on the lake. She was desperate to play friends. She'd brought buns, coffee, proper napkins ... It was all quite nice, but I'd only managed a few strokes before she started with the usual digs about stepping up in various situations – meaning that evening's dinner, in other words, she wanted me to make an effort. Which ultimately meant she wanted me to ignore how I felt and keep up the facade ... She really is a fucking bitch.'

# 27

They rounded off the foresters' day celebrations with a strong coffee and a slice of princesstårta in the grand dining room at the manor before all going their separate ways. The table was cleared, the chairs pushed in and the room left quiet once again.

After trying to reach André's girlfriend Frida for the third time, Julia went out into the narrow service hallway to wait for Amelie.

The only people with a confirmed alibi for three o'clock on the day of the shareholders' meeting were Monika and Siri. Someone other than Frida might still corroborate André's account, but Björn and PG had been clear: they were alone at the time when Werther died.

Amelie made her way over to the dresser with an armful of clean tablecloths and starched napkins. A brief flicker of fear passed over her face when she saw Julia, but she quickly composed herself.

Julia found herself thinking that Amelie was used to being invisible, which made her particularly exposed and vulnerable whenever she came into focus.

'I don't want to keep you, but I was hoping we could have a quick chat,' she said. 'Where were you at three o'clock on the afternoon of the shareholders' meeting?'

'I was here, preparing dinner,' Amelie replied, stacking the tablecloths on the shelf in the cabinet.

'Did you see anyone else?'

The housekeeper opened one of the drawers, placed the napkins inside and then straightened up.

'See? I baked some sweet buns and packed Monika's picnic basket. That was just before two, and I seized the chance to discuss the evening's menu with her, because the langoustines we'd ordered hadn't arrived.'

'And after that?'

'I laid the table, started cooking. PG got back from the forest just before four. He was hungry and wanted frikadeller and beer. I got a delivery of veal at five, and Monika came back with the Thermos and the dirty cups at around the same time.'

'Did she say anything?'

'She just washed her hands and moaned that the boat was getting rusty.'

'Nothing about Siri?'

'Not that I'd care to pass on,' Amelie replied.

'How long have you been working here at Mannheim?'

'Thirty years. I was brought in to help with Siri's confirmation, and I was given a permanent job after that.'

'What was your first impression of the family?'

Amelie paused briefly, and her eyes narrowed as she considered her answer. 'I remember thinking that Werther was Siri's father,' she replied with a smile. 'Because he was the one who gave the speech during the party, and he also gave her the gift from the rest of the family.'

'Her mother's diamond ring?'

'Yes,' Amelie replied, lowering her eyes.

'I understand you weren't particularly fond of Werther?' Julia pressed on, studying Amelie closely.

'One shouldn't speak ill of the dead, but he could be hard work – particularly if he'd been drinking,' she replied quietly.

'No one seems to have liked him, but from what I've seen so far he isn't the only one who can be rude and aggressive ...'

'That's true.'

'What was it about Werther in particular that you didn't like?'

Amelie's face remained blank, but Julia noticed that her hands were shaking as she lifted another stack of napkins into the drawer.

'What happened?' Julia asked her.

'What do you mean?'

'You took time off whenever he came to visit.'

Amelie closed the drawer and turned to Julia. Her eyes had darkened, and angry red blotches had flared up on her cheeks.

'Werther behaved the way the rich always have around the working class. But I was strong enough to stand up for myself when the time came.'

'Good for you,' said Julia.

'He came into the kitchen drunk out of his mind and told me he thought I cost too much, that there should be other perks included in the price ... I was busy cutting celery at the time, so I just ignored him ... But he came up behind me, pushed me against the counter and reached under my skirt. Well, I turned around with the knife in my hand and ... then I went through to Monika in the study and told her that her brother-in-law had hurt himself, that he probably needed an ambulance. No one ever mentioned it again, but Monika always accepted my request for leave whenever Werther came to visit.'

'Did you hate him?' Julia asked.

'I wouldn't say that.'

'Is there anyone who didn't dislike Werther?'

Amelie's tense face softened. 'Siri, I suppose.'

'Why?'

'She was the youngest of the children, and Werther was always on her side. He kept coming to visit on her birthday, too. I don't know why, but that made me happy. I've always felt a bit sorry for Siri.'

'Why is that?'

Amelie lowered her voice. 'No one cared about her. She was practically neglected, or so I've heard. Her mother Cecilia used to—'

The floor creaked, and Amelie immediately stopped talking. The two women turned around and saw that André was watching them from the doorway.

'What were you about to say?' asked Julia.

'No, nothing,' Amelie mumbled, hurrying back through to the kitchen.

Julia stacked the last few napkins in the drawer, and as she pushed it shut she felt André approaching from behind. She turned around just as he reached her, leaning in to the dresser with one hand on either side of her head.

She looked him straight in the eye, and he stared back at her with catlike calm. Julia's cane clattered to the floor. Her legs felt like jelly, and she broke out in a sweat.

'You should go home, you're done here. The police are in charge now,' he said with a joyless smile.

Julia's chin began to tremble, and she was powerless to hold back the tears. The fear of being touched was so strong that she couldn't move a muscle. She wanted to ask him to leave her alone, but she couldn't manage a single word.

André studied her calmly, then leaned in and gave her a quick peck on the lips before turning and walking away.

Julia slumped to the floor and clutched her face, rubbing her mouth repeatedly until she managed to shake off the feeling of torn body parts on her lips. Slowly but surely, she regained her composure, dried her cheeks and used her stick to get to her feet.

Her breathing was still ragged as she made her way through to the entrance hall, opened the front door and continued out onto the steps, filling her lungs with cool air. André was already over by the lake, walking slowly along the edge of the police cordon. It was a sunny day, and she could see pollen and insects floating through the air in the bright light.

Julia hurried down the steps and out onto the raked gravel, over to André's silver Porsche. Her arms were shaking as she raised her titanium cane and used it to smash the windscreen. She brought the handle down on the bonnet, hitting it repeatedly until there was a deep dent. She then shattered the headlights and made her way around the side of the car to turn her attention to the doors.

Right then, she noticed that Siri was watching her with wide eyes from the window of the Red Room.

Julia stopped, short of breath. She waved, then used the stick to smash the side window, dent another door and break the rear lights.

# 28

Julia was out of breath, her entire body trembling as she climbed the steps into the entrance hall. She continued through the drawing room, past the gleaming grand piano and the bar in the study, thinking about what Amelie had said about Siri being neglected as a child.

The slightly sweet scent of old books hit her as she stepped into the Red Room.

Siri was sitting in one of the armchairs with a bar of chocolate and a thick paperback in her lap. She was wearing a white knitted sweater and wide-legged trousers, a pair of slippers on her delicate feet.

'What happened?' she asked calmly, lowering her reading glasses to the table.

'There was an accident with André's car,' Julia replied.

'My dear brother smiles a lot, but he's not always the kindest of men.'

'Something like that,' said Julia.

'Are the two of you even now?'

Julia ignored the question and sat down in the armchair opposite Siri, reaching up to smooth her hair. Her forehead was damp.

'George Saunders,' she said, nodding at the book in Siri's lap. 'What do you make of it?'

'It's good. Very different,' said Siri.

'I love his ghosts,' Julia said with a smile, resting her cane across her knees.

'I know ...' Siri laughed, which made her face light up, a flash of mischievousness and youth. 'Help yourself to the chocolate if you'd like some.'

'Thank you,' said Julia, gazing out through the tall leaded windows.

The bright morning light made the pines outside look unnaturally green. The dead flies on the windowsill shifted slightly in the draught.

'It's good for the heart.'

'Certain women seem to have felt trapped here at Mannheim,' said Julia, changing the subject.

'Isn't that true of women everywhere?'

'I've heard you had a bit of a hard time as a child?' Julia pressed on, turning to look at Siri.

'Who told you that?'

'You were the youngest of five children and also the only girl,' Julia continued, ignoring the question.

'I had to grow a thick skin.'

'How did that work out?'

Siri massaged the back of her neck. 'Pretty well, I think ... Though most of the time no one paid any attention to me. They were all too preoccupied with themselves; I was too young.'

'So you were quite lonely?'

She shrugged. 'I had friends at school, did gymnastics ...'

'Your parents both worked for the company?'
'Yes, at first.'
'What happened?'
Siri sighed. 'Dad drank and Mum had migraines.'
Julia nodded. 'What was that like for you?'
'They could be gone for days at a time, sometimes even longer,' she said.
'Who took care of you, then?'
'No one. I mean, I got by, the way children do.'
'That sounds quite unusual.'
'Werther sometimes came over with food, filled the fridge.' Siri's eyes welled up at the memory.
'But who ... How can I put this ... who made sure you were in clean clothes, that you brushed your hair and washed and went to bed on time?'
'It wasn't like that,' said Siri.
'No?'
'I looked after myself, and I enjoyed it. It made me feel grown up, like I could do anything ... Go to bed whenever I wanted.'
'Your mother can't have had migraines all the time?'
'No,' said Siri, looking away.
'What were things like when she was feeling well?'
Something troubled flickered over Siri's face. 'She never felt well. She had severe depression, migraines were just what she called the worst periods.'
It was clear she was starting to find the conversation difficult. Her voice grew flat, and a deep crease had appeared on her forehead.

'How did you deal with her low moods?' asked Julia.

'It was a bit worse than that ...'

'I understand, but I'm wondering ... Did you feel like you had a responsibility to look after her?'

Siri gave Julia a confused glance. 'What?'

'Some children almost take on a parenting role, if you understand what I mean.'

'No, I didn't do anything. She couldn't stand me. Whenever she was in one of her black holes I had to stay away. She hated me, completely ignored me.'

'Did she have postnatal depression?'

Siri broke off a piece of chocolate. 'That's what I've always assumed, not that it was ever given a name ... It was a vicious circle. Mum's illness made Dad drink more, and his drinking made her sink even deeper. Honestly, their marriage was fucking awful. It got ground down, simple as that.' Her eyes welled up as she spoke, tears spilling down her cheeks. 'I don't know whether Mum developed some form of dementia. I did everything I could not to bother her. The minute she saw me, she started screaming and throwing things at me.'

She popped a piece of chocolate in her mouth, dried her cheeks and smiled in an attempt to downplay the gravity of the situation.

'What would she shout?'

'I don't know, I can't remember. Don't want to think about it. She ended up being committed when I was ten, to round-the-clock care ... I only went to see her once, but she was heavily medicated and didn't even recognise me.'

'That must have been hard on you.'

'I had André and Björn.'

'Still ... A mother is important.'

'I know she loved me deep down,' Siri said, as though she was talking to herself.

'Yes,' Julia said quietly, getting to her feet.

She went over to the bar cart to get a napkin, handing it to Siri the same way Sid had with Monika. 'Though I know that's a lie,' Siri mumbled, blowing her nose. 'It's just something you tell yourself.'

Julia sat down again. 'What about your father?'

'I think he loved me too, but he was weak. He couldn't do anything about Mum, he just went through to the kitchen and started drinking whenever she got going. When things were really bad I'd come over here, to see PG and Werther.'

'What was their family like?'

'Not so great either.'

'Do you remember when PG and Werther's mother committed suicide?'

She shook her head and blew her nose again. 'I was too young, just a baby.'

'What happened? Do you know?'

'No,' Siri replied, getting to her feet.

# 29

After lunch, PG went off to attend to some business in the forest and Monika headed over to Sundsvall to visit her hairdresser, leaving Julia and Sid alone in the enormous house. Not even Amelie was around; she had gone to pick up the rug from the dry cleaner.

'Opportunity makes the thief,' said Sid.

Julia followed him as he left the entrance hall and made his way over to the grand piano in the drawing room. He got down on his knees by the stool, and she watched as he squinted and took out a pair of tweezers. Sid picked up a long strand of blonde hair from the velvet cushion and dropped it into an evidence tube.

They then continued down the hallway to PG and Monika's private suite at the end of the house facing the forest.

Julia kept watch as Sid nipped inside. The sliding doors rolled shut behind him, knocking into each other with an eerie thud.

She turned around and peered back down the corridor, past the office.

The dark panels on the wall shone dully in the glow of the sconces. Julia took a few steps forward and opened a narrow door held shut with a latch. The little box room on the other side was messy, a jumble of old boots, umbrellas, life jackets, raincoats and boxes of old toys.

She saw a small cowboy hat with a silver star on the front, a plastic Tyrannosaurus rex with a chewed tail, a Big Jim doll and a bucket of blue Smurfs. Toys from a childhood half a century ago.

She moved back over to the sliding doors, thinking about the strange absence of children or young people at Mannheim. No one from the current generation had kids, Monika had told her.

The house was as good as silent, the only sound coming from the soft creaking of the parquet floor as the temperature shifted. It almost sounded like someone was dropping nut casings to the floor.

Yet again, Julia found herself thinking about the fact that PG's mother had taken her own life and that Siri seemed to have developed some form of reactive depressive psychosis. The strange coincidence that both mothers had suffered serious mental health problems – assuming the underlying causes weren't the same for both women, she thought.

Their marriages had both been utterly catastrophic, by the sounds of it.

Julia dropped that thought as she suddenly saw herself from the outside. She had ruined her own marriage, and now she had hired her ex in a desperate attempt to keep him in her life.

She heard a car pull up on the gravel outside, and she turned around and pushed the sliding doors open a fraction.

'Sid?' she hissed, trying to keep her voice low. 'Come back! Now!'

She tried to listen for him, but she couldn't hear a single sound from inside the suite.

The car door closed outside, and Julia's heart began to race. 'Sid!'

Julia let go of the heavy doors, letting them roll shut. She used the tip of her cane to try to dampen the sound, but the brief rumble of wood on wood was like a distant clap of thunder.

She hurried back down the hallway, stopping to listen when the front door opened.

Julia heard footsteps heading through to the kitchen, followed by the clattering of a pot.

She kept going, coming out into the entrance hall at the same time as Amelie. The older woman was standing with a pan lid in one hand.

'Ah, there you are,' said Julia, trying to seem pleasantly surprised. 'I've been looking for you all over.'

'I had to go to the dry cleaner.'

'Of course, I forgot ... Sid has a migraine and needs some sort of painkiller before—'

She trailed off as Sidney came strolling out into the hall, stopping dead when he spotted them.

'I was just telling Amelie about your migraine. Did you find anything?'

'No, I ... I didn't want to intrude,' he said, pressing his fingertips to his left eye.

'What kind of pills do you need?' Amelie asked, a slight note of hesitancy in her voice.

'Anything will do.'

'PG usually takes Naproxen the day after.'

'Great,' Sid groaned.

They followed her back down the corridor and into PG's office. The tall trees outside blocked out much of the light, giving the room a subdued, cosy feel. Julia noticed a pale grey projector on a stand beside a box of film.

Amelie walked straight around the desk, opened the top drawer and took out a pack of pills. Her eyes scanned the text on the back, then she put it back and took out another carton, handing it to Sid. 'I'll get you some water.'

He thanked her and popped one of the pills out into his hand.

Amelie lifted the heavy jug of water on the desk and poured him a glass.

'Is PG having a film screening?' Julia asked as Sid swallowed the medicine.

'He's been planning to digitise some of the family films,' Amelie explained.

'Gustav VI Adolf,' Julia read from the roll in the projector.

'Yes, the King came here in 1956, for the hundredth anniversary of the Mannheim company.'

'Wow.'

'Sylvester was awarded His Majesty's gold medal for outstanding services to the country.'

'Hey, you don't have one of those, Sid,' Julia joked.

He didn't reply, just stood quietly with his fingers still pressed to his eye.

'I think PG was planning to show you the film, but . . . Well, with everything that's happened, I suppose he never got round to it.'

'Could we watch it now?' asked Julia.

'I'm not sure . . .'

'That would be fun, wouldn't it, Sid?'

'Sure,' he replied with a plucky smile.

Amelie went over to the window and drew the curtains, as though she had been planning the film screening all along. Julia turned on the projector, waited until it had reached full brightness, and then set the film rolling, adjusting the focus as the first images came into view.

The black and white footage began with a soundless panorama of people arriving at Mannheim in ballgowns and tailcoats.

Julia, Sid and Amelie stood in the darkened room, watching images from the past that had been caught on a strip of celluloid. The film rattled through the gate.

With the flick of a switch, people who were no longer alive filled the lavish halls of Mannheim once again.

The projector fan whirred, giving off the scent of hot metal.

'That's Sylvester,' Amelie said quietly.

The suit-clad man looked just like PG, only with an icy gaze and fuller lips. He was standing behind a small podium, talking to an older man with a moustache and a large stomach.

'And Linnea.'

A young woman turned to Sylvester, a trace of laughter still lingering on her face from the conversation she had just finished.

'She's beautiful,' Julia whispered.

Linnea had her hair pinned up beneath a silver tiara studded with pearls. She was wearing a long silk dress with a fitted bodice, a pearl necklace and a diamond ring on the hand resting on Sylvester's arm.

The camera angle changed abruptly, showing the guests now standing in line along the walls of the hall. The King and his entourage arrived, walking between the two rows of people and pausing in front of the stage where Sylvester was waiting.

Gustaf VI Adolf was wearing a navy dress uniform with two stars pinned to the chest, trousers featuring a gold stripe, a shirt and a black bow-tie.

He had to be over seventy, his grey hair neatly combed to one side, black-rimmed glasses and a confused, absent look on his face.

The first adjutant and eight chief adjutants came together as the Marshal of the Realm opened a glossy wooden box, handed it to the King and then, with reserved movements, climbed the steps and stood beside Sylvester.

The King said something to Sylvester Mott and handed over the box containing the medal. The two men then shook hands with a surprising degree of intensity, exchanged another few words and then turned to face the guests.

A brass band seemed to play a fanfare, everyone stood tall, and then the film came to an end. The screen went white, and the strip of film flapped loosely.

# 30

WERTHER'S LEGAL REPRESENTATIVE HAD BEEN called to a meeting to take the family through his last will and testament. Julia and Sid had requested to be present, and were now sitting by the wall in the dining room as the Motts gathered around the big dining table.

André marched over to them and looked Julia straight in the eye. 'I'll be filing a police report, just so you know,' he snarled.

'I'm not sure I understand.'

'You wrecked my car.'

'What?' she asked, feigning surprise. 'Why would I do that?'

Moving impatiently, Björn guided his wheelchair into the dining room. The wheels left dusty tyre tracks on the parquet floor. Siri got up and pulled out a chair to make space for him.

André turned away from Julia and sat down beside his brother.

PG came over instead, studying Sid with a look of concern. 'How are you feeling?' he asked.

'Much better, thank you.'

'Glad to hear it,' said PG, walking over to take his seat with downcast eyes.

Monika handed out notepads and pens, and Amelie came in with a large tray of food – scones, pastries and canapés – which she set down on the table. Monika thanked her and then turned to the others.

'Help yourselves, everyone,' she said quietly.

Björn leaned forward and did as he was told.

At the sound of quick footsteps approaching the dining room, all heads turned to the doorway.

The lawyer made a quietly dignified entrance. She was a tall woman in her thirties, wearing a navy blue skirt suit and a bronze silk blouse. She had glossy, shoulder-length black hair, amber eyes and a serious mouth.

'Welcome to Mannheim,' said PG.

'Thank you,' she replied, taking a seat.

'Go on then, tear the plaster off,' Björn mumbled.

The lawyer placed her briefcase on the table on front of her and straightened her chair.

'It has long been custom in this family to write a will in a timely manner, to prevent the division of the estate if there are no direct heirs,' she began, nodding in thanks as Amelie served the tea.

'My mother would have inherited from my father before we were born,' PG confirmed. 'And Monika stands to inherit from me. Sylvester made sure that—'

'Who cares?' Björn interjected. 'I just want to know what Werther's will says.'

'He wasn't married and had no direct heirs,' the lawyer continued.

'We know! What the hell is this?' Björn laughed, looking around in search of support.

'Per Günter is his closest relative, which means he would have inherited everything if Werther hadn't prepared a will,' she said calmly, taking an envelope out of her bag and opening it.

'But clearly he did,' said André, running a hand through his hair.

'Yes,' she said, placing two stapled sheets of watermarked paper on the table. 'This will was made seven years ago, signed by Werther Mott, notarised by us and filed in accordance with all regulations. The only slightly unusual feature, which doesn't change anything in substance, is that the will begins with a statement. One that Werther instructed us to read aloud.'

'OK,' André sighed.

The lawyer cleared her throat. 'That statement is as follows: "I once read a letter that stole my soul."'

There was a brief silence around the table.

'What the fuck is that supposed to mean?' Björn snapped after a moment.

'His soul?' PG whispered.

'Could we get on with the will now?' asked Monika.

'Yes,' said the lawyer. 'Werther left his shares, property and all personal effects to one person. Siri Mott.'

'What the hell did you just say?' PG barked.

'I'm just trying—'

Monika dropped her cup, which shattered on the floor. Shards of china scattered across the parquet.

'I'm just trying to share what's written in the will,' the lawyer replied.

Siri flinched as PG brought his palm down on the table. Björn leaned back in his chair with his hands to his face.

'I can't believe this,' Monika shouted. 'Why would he—'

'Blackmail,' PG cut her off.

'Please ... stop,' Siri begged them, eyes welling up.

'What the fuck have you done, Siri?' PG asked, his voice wavering. 'You're going to have to explain this. You know that, don't you?'

'I have no idea,' she whispered, shaking her head.

'She must have tricked him,' said Monika.

'No, I swear,' Siri sobbed. 'I didn't ask for any of this, I'm just as shocked as the rest of you ...'

'If you could all calm down for a moment,' said the lawyer, 'then I can go through—'

'This is nonsense,' Monika interrupted her. 'We dispute the will. This goes against everything Sylvester stood for – Leopold and Mannheim, too.'

Siri had clamped a hand to her mouth.

'Werther always felt sorry for Siri, but not *this* damn sorry,' said PG. 'If she inherits his thirty-five per cent then her existing ten per cent will make her the majority shareholder.'

'I'll be damned,' André mumbled.

'Man, I don't understand shit,' Björn said with a grin.

'Hold on a moment,' the lawyer spoke up, raising her voice. 'We're talking about a share of twenty-five per cent.'

'I beg your fucking pardon?' said PG.

The lawyer stood up and leaned forward with both hands on the table. 'Would you mind letting me finish?'

The murmur died down, and the five pale faces turned to her again. Monika's lips were pressed tightly together.

'Werther owned twenty-five per cent of Mannheim at the time of his death. He recently transferred ten per cent to Björn,' she explained.

'What is this? A coup?' PG asked, turning to his cousins.

'He got in touch with me and wanted to compensate Björn for the back injury,' André replied, sounding stressed.

'That doesn't sound like my brother,' said PG.

'We contest that too,' said Monika. 'Werther must have been mentally unstable if he—'

'What the hell are you talking about?' André practically screamed. 'You don't know a thing! You shouldn't even be here. Can't we send them all out before we—'

'Shut up, André,' PG snapped.

# 31

THE MOTTS ALL WENT THEIR separate ways after the fractious meeting, and Julia and Sid chose to eat dinner in his room at the end of the corridor on the first floor. They had set out the food Amelie had cooked – fried zander, chips and remoulade – on the round table by the big window looking out onto the chapel and the old mill. The sky was clear, the full moon glittering in the water. The presence of the forest felt like dense matter, the existence of something ancient and alien.

Julia was painfully aware that she still hadn't told Sid about her plans to recruit him to her detective agency, but she also didn't want to ruin the moment, this brief time they had together. She was afraid he would be upset and turn her down if she was too rash. As things stood, her plan was to solve this case – ideally dazzling him in the process – before she broached the subject and suggested he took a six-month sabbatical from the police force to see whether it felt like a good fit.

'Such drama,' Sid said with a sigh, pouring more wine into their glasses.

'Everyone seemed genuinely surprised by Werther's will,' said Julia, eating a crispy piece of fish.

'I know. Who do you think was most surprised?' he asked, studying her.

'Siri, maybe?' she replied, kicking off her pumps beneath the table.

Sid's eyes narrowed, the way they always did when he was thinking.

'I thought Monika and PG seemed most taken aback,' he said.

'PG totally lost it,' she nodded.

'Did you notice how the others reacted?'

'Yes. André was annoyed with Monika. But before that, while he was listening to the lawyer, all he said was "I'll be damned." Sighing, almost, as though he understood why but hadn't quite expected it to actually happen.'

'What about Björn?'

'He just lowered his head to his hands,' she replied, coating a couple of chips in sauce.

'Did he?'

'Yup.'

Julia sipped her wine and replayed her memories of each of their faces as the lawyer went through the will. Siri's eyes had widened in surprise. PG's face had paled, and he had ended up with saliva on his bottom lip when he lost his temper. Monika's jaw had tensed so hard that her temple began to twitch.

'We already knew that Werther had signed over ten per cent to Björn two weeks before he died,' said Sid, 'but the real bombshell was that Siri stood to inherit the remaining twenty-five, and—'

'I can't help but smile,' said Julia. 'The second cousins suddenly have the majority. The King dies, and power is shared.'

Sid drank a little more wine, lowered his glass and used his thumb to wipe his mouth.

'The will was made seven years ago, which means we can probably assume Werther was compos mentis at the time, that it was what he wanted,' he said. 'He didn't have a wife or kids. The only person he really seems to have cared about was Siri, so it seems pretty logical that she'd inherit his estate.'

'Yes ...'

'What did you make of the statement?'

'I once read a letter that stole my soul,' Julia quoted from memory.

'What do you think it means?'

'Good question,' she replied, as much to herself as anything.

Julia lifted her glass to drink, but she paused as a thought came to her. She stared blankly ahead for a moment or two without a word.

'What are you thinking?' Sid eventually asked.

'I'm putting the pieces together.'

'Is it almost time to get everyone together in the library?'

'Tomorrow at the latest ... There's just one last thing I need to do,' she replied.

Sid smiled. 'Who's it pointing to?'

Julia realised she was still holding her wine glass, the glow of the ceiling light mirrored in the trembling red liquid.

'I started thinking about the fact that Björn endured years of Werther's cruelty, contempt ... even the abuse that put him in a wheelchair. When André pushed for compensation, that could have been the final straw.'

'Björn, then.'

'No matter which way I look at it, I just keep coming back to him.'

'Even though it's impossible, because he couldn't have taken PG's phone from the service corridor in his wheelchair.'

'The photograph is the joker in the pack, the coincidence that set this whole investigation in motion. There are several possible explanations, but the most likely must be some variant of PG's theory. He was drunk and on medication, just like he told us, staggering around outside just before twelve – we have two witnesses who back that up. He could have been checking on the property out of some sense of duty . . . Let's say he was wandering about in the darkness when he noticed that the light was on in the brewhouse and went over there to see what was going on. He could have seen Werther's body and taken a picture, only he was so drunk he forgot the plan on the way back . . . And when he woke the next day, he didn't remember a thing.'

'But his phone was back on the dresser the next morning,' Sid pointed out.

'We don't actually know that for sure. It could just be something PG told us to cover himself. I mean, he couldn't have known that Werther had already been dead for over eight hours by the time he took the picture.'

'So, what? You think Björn was humiliated by the deal?' asked Sid, spearing a couple of chips on his fork.

'He makes no secret of the fact that he hates Werther, which you might expect him to do if he was actually guilty.'

'At least if he's worried about being caught,' said Sid.

'Exactly, but I really don't think he is,' she said. 'He's brusque, but he also has a sense of justice. He doesn't think a person should be able to buy their way out of their guilt ... Werther injured Björn, André negotiated and Werther paid up. Not out of regret, not because it was the right or reasonable thing to do, but because he wanted to avoid a scandal. But the way I see it, Björn would have *preferred* a scandal. He doesn't care about the shares; he wanted to drag everything out into the light, all the years of ... of disparity.'

'But André convinced his brother to accept the deal,' said Sid. 'Which is understandable, really. It's a huge sum of money.'

'Yes, but I think Björn could have changed his mind and arranged to meet Werther one-on-one, either to talk to him or to punish him.'

'Björn was the only one who knew Werther was coming to the meeting,' Sid said with a nod.

'We have no idea what he was planning, but Werther – who probably thought he'd already been more than generous – took a taxi from the station to the brewhouse, where Björn stored his renovation projects and his tools.'

'The preliminary autopsy report mentions blunt force trauma, a single blow to the head with an object that didn't leave any particles. That could definitely be one of his tools, something like a sledgehammer.'

'Björn has a strong upper body, no doubt about it. He could've waited for Werther, accused him and then killed him – whether intentionally or not.'

'Which means it was probably him you saw from your window when the fire first started,' said Sid. 'That could fit, but I can't quite work out how a man in a wheelchair could manage to sink a body in the lake, even if he is strong.'

'I have a theory.'

'Care to share it?'

'Soon,' Julia said with a smile.

'You know you're not always right, don't you?'

# 32

The evening drinks were due to start in a quarter of an hour, so Julia left Sid's room to go and get changed. The thick Persian carpet dulled the sound of her cane as she walked down the corridor. She paused outside her door, turned the key and shuddered as she stepped into the darkness inside. While her hand groped for the switch on the wall, she was overcome by the chill and the compact silence among the mangled bodies.

The switch clicked and light filled the room, gleaming like a warped sun in the dark windows.

Her handbag was on the floor by her feet.

She hadn't noticed that she had dropped it.

Using her cane to support herself, she bent down and pushed everything back inside. Lipstick, keys, tampons, her card holder.

Julia left her cane propped up against the bed and went through to the bathroom to do her make-up once her hands had stopped shaking.

Björn was the only member of the family who had known that Werther was definitely planning to attend the meeting, she thought as she opened her toiletry bag. But even if the others had known, they wouldn't have been surprised if he had failed to show up. Werther was a recluse, and no one would have missed him. Siri was possibly the only exception to that, once her birthday came around, but probably not enough to worry.

Björn hadn't known that a photograph had been taken before he dumped the body in the lake.

Julia leaned in to the mirror and used concealer to hide her scar as best she could. She powdered her face and applied some lipstick, then added a little blusher to her cheeks and turned her attention to her eyes, not stopping until she caught a glimpse of her mother's face in hers.

'Do you think the killer was expecting an investigation?' she asked her reflection.

If Werther's body hadn't floated up to the surface by the dam, if there hadn't been a picture on PG's phone, then there wouldn't have been an investigation. At most, there might have been a missing person's inquiry in a few years' time.

Julia added a few drops of perfume to her wrists and throat, put her hair up and then took her long green silk dress with an open back out of the wardrobe.

\* \* \*

Both freshened up, Julia and Sid made their way down the stairs, through the dining room, to the study. Melancholy jazz music was playing over the old gramophone.

Monika and PG were dancing, rocking slowly back and forth. He was wearing a creased tuxedo and a burgundy silk scarf,

Monika a greyish-blue cocktail dress, long gloves and a two-strand pearl necklace.

André was behind the bar with a cocktail shaker. He had a five o'clock shadow and was wearing a pinstripe suit, his hair slicked back. Siri was sitting on one of the tall stools in front of him in a black sequin dress with fringing at the hem, a black velvet ribbon and flower around her neck. Björn was wearing a bow-tie, his white shirt straining over his belly.

The music died down, and PG let go of Monika, staggered over to the gramophone and turned the record. The speakers crackled as he picked a fleck of dust from the needle.

The sound of a solitary cornet with a damper filled the room, brushes sweeping over a snare drum.

Monika spotted Sid and Julia, and she welcomed them in with a drunken smile, telling them to take a seat at the bar so that she could make them both a drink.

'The new ownership structure means we have no way of stopping the sale of Mannheim now,' she explained, dropping a few ice cubes into a shaker. 'We'll lose the house, be forced to leave our home ...'

'It'll be OK,' PG said softly.

He leaned against the bar, using a spoon to scoop a few peanuts from a silver bowl and tip them into his cupped hand. One by one, he popped them into his mouth.

'The old world is coming to an end, and we're celebrating its dying moments,' Monika continued, unscrewing the lid of a bottle of gin.

'Oddly enough, I don't seem to be shedding a tear,' said André.

'I just feel so sad about everything,' Siri mumbled, pressing a gentle finger to the skin beneath her eyes.

'That's because you can afford to,' Monika snapped back.
'Fuck you, Monika.'
'Well said,' she replied, handing Julia her drink.
'Siri, why do you think Werther failed to mention that he'd left you everything?' Julia asked, lowering the glass to the counter.

Siri turned to her with dark, teary eyes. 'I don't know. I honestly have no idea.'

'PG? What do you think?'

'That I should hurry up and drink all the booze before we lose that too,' he said, pouring himself another whisky.

'Just another day of grifting for the great detectives,' André said with a smile, fixing his eyes on Julia. 'Dinners, parties ... A cocktail in the study.'

'We're extremely grateful for the generosity we've been shown here,' she replied, keeping her voice neutral.

'But you'll still expect to be paid.'

'Don't be so rude,' said Monika, her mouth taut.

'This is my job ... Listening, decoding,' said Julia.

'And it's going well, is it?' asked André.

'Yes.'

'Is this where you get us all together and point out the killer?'

'Maybe.'

André ignored Björn, who held up his own empty glass for a refill as he poured himself another. Siri ate the olive from hers and then dropped the cocktail stick into her glass.

'Björn, Werther signed over ten per cent of the shares to you, as compensation,' said Sid.

'Yup,' he confirmed. He stretched as far as he could, his fingers only just reaching the carafe of whisky on the bar.

'You must be relieved that it all worked out?'

'The hell are you on about?' he asked, pouring himself a drink.

Without a word, André snatched the bottle from him. PG rubbed his eye, smearing kohl across his cheek before he started shaking a dented brass shaker.

'By Swedish standards, it was a pretty big sum that—'

'He didn't buy my silence, if that's what you're suggesting. I'll never stop saying that he was a real bastard,' Björn snapped, knocking back his whisky.

'This is why we have family dinners, so we can scream and shout at each other,' Monika explained to Sid.

'From the outside, us Motts look as perfect as we always have,' Björn continued, his eyes still on Sid. 'Because if you can't keep up the facade, you might as well put a bullet in your brain, hang yourself, throw yourself in the river or stick your head in the oven . . .'

PG tried to pour Siri a drink, but she covered her glass with her hand. He turned away from her, swigged direct from the shaker and then wiped his mouth and chin with his hand.

'Take it easy, honey,' Monika whispered, reaching out to touch his back.

André's neck seemed stiff as he poured aged rum into his grappa glass. Björn had spilled whisky on his shirt, and Siri got up and left the room, eyes downcast.

'Time for the truth to come out,' PG slurred.

'Yes,' said Julia.

'Christ, I almost feel like confessing myself, just to get rid of the two of you,' André said with a smile, raising his glass to her.

Monika propped herself up on her elbows and closed her eyes. PG drank the last of the cocktail from the shaker and then bent down to get more ice from the freezer. As he straightened up, he lost his balance and fell. The ice scattered across the parquet.

Sid hurried over to help Monika get him back onto his feet.

'You OK to stand?' he asked, an arm around PG's shoulders.

'He's fine,' said Monika.

Sid reluctantly let go.

'What the hell just happened?' PG groaned.

'Go and lie down,' Monika told him.

'I'm fine.'

'Just do as I say.'

PG ran a hand over his hair, grabbed Monika's glass from the bar and knocked it back. He then turned to Sid and Julia.

'My dear wife is afraid I'll embarrass myself, but don't you worry. I'm a good boy, I'll go up to bed.'

'Do you need any help?' asked Monika.

'No, for chrissakes, just look after our guests.'

His shirt had come untucked from his waistband, but his silk scarf was still elegantly tied as he staggered around the bar.

'Is he going already?' Björn mumbled, squinting after his second cousin.

PG paused in the doorway, bracing himself against the frame. He looked like he wanted to turn around and come back, but he changed his mind and went on his way.

Monika gave Sid a top up and then toasted with him. André sipped his rum and tried to catch Julia's eye.

'What is it?' she asked.

'Do you have a murder weapon? Prints? DNA? You've got nothing, have you?'

Piano music drifted through from the drawing room, tinkling notes. Siri had sat down at the grand piano.

'Almost feels like the old days,' Monika said with a smile.

André grabbed his glass and walked off in the direction of the music. Monika said something inaudible and then ushered Sid after him.

Julia took the stopper out of the carafe of whisky, poured herself a measure and then put the carafe on one of the shelves. Björn was sitting with his eyes closed, and she couldn't tell whether he was asleep or simply listening to the music.

Siri started playing the third movement of Chopin's Piano Sonata No. 2, the oddly enticing funeral march.

Julia sipped her whisky and walked away from the music, into the gloom of the Red Room. The deep red Persian rug was back, its kaleidoscopic pattern almost three-dimensional. The air smelled like wood and old books, and she paused in the doorway and glanced back into the study, where Björn was still slumped in his wheelchair.

As she was watching him, his eyes snapped open and he turned his chair towards the drawing room.

Julia took a step to one side so that he wouldn't see her.

Björn wheeled back around, pushing the joystick with both hands and making his way over to the bar, where he set his glass down on the edge.

He glanced around and then groaned in pain as he stood up and took an unsteady step forward, snatching the carafe of whisky from the shelf before slumping back into his chair.

Julia left her hiding place and walked back towards him. Björn looked up at her, filled his glass and then drank as he leaned back.

'A classic, huh?' he said.

'Is there anything you want to tell me?' she asked, pausing in front of him.

'André thought I should ham up the injury a bit,' he replied.

'I think you killed Werther.'

'You do, do you?'

'I think you're a cruel blackmailer and a killer.'

Julia raised her glass to him in a toast, took a sip and then put it down.

'But can you prove it?'

'I'm calling the police right now.'

'I should probably get ready, then,' he said, pouring himself another whisky and drinking.

'I'm prepared to be discreet if you cooperate.'

'Is this where I deny any wrongdoing ... or should I be calling a lawyer?'

'Björn, many people feel a sense of relief when they finally come clean,' she continued.

He sighed deeply and loosened his bow-tie. 'It's far more complicated than you can imagine,' he said, fixing his eyes on his half-full glass.

'I'm listening.'

'Nope ... You call the police.'

'I hope they drag you out of here kicking and screaming,' she said, taking out her phone.

## 33

Julia had called the police and asked them to make an arrest when the sound of piano died down. Björn had just poured his third whisky, the glass resting on his rounded belly as he sat with his eyes closed. She heard quiet applause, followed by the creaking of the floor, and Sid came back into the study.

'So this is where you're hiding, is it?'

'We need to talk,' she said.

André laughed loudly at something. He appeared in the doorway and waved dismissively to the others. 'We're all th-th-thirstyyyy,' he sang, making his way over to the bar.

Monika followed him in, but she stopped dead as though she was in pain, a hand to her pearl necklace and her eyes closed. Siri came in and stood beside her. The thin black fringing on the hem of her dress swung around her legs.

'Coffee?' she asked quietly.

Monika turned to her and put a hand on her cheek, in what looked like a genuine mark of affection.

Siri smiled weakly, turned away and walked off towards the kitchen.

Monika's phone pinged, and she dug it out of her clutch and checked the display. 'Oh, God,' she gasped.

Julia gripped her cane and moved over to her. 'What's wrong?'

'Nothing, it's just PG ... I thought he was going to bed ...'

'What has he sent?'

'It's nothing.'

'Would you show me?'

With a sigh, Monika held up the picture PG had just sent her. On the wet bathroom floor beside a vomit-streaked toilet, she could see PG's silk scarf, a half-empty bottle of gin, a pack of painkillers, an old key and a large amount of unrolled toilet paper.

'Looks like he wants me to go and check on him,' she said.

'Could you forward that picture to me?' asked Julia.

Her phone pinged as the message arrived.

Monika hurried off towards the stairs, and Sid put down his glass and came over to Julia with a confused look on his face.

'I've called the police. It's time for them to take Björn in for questioning,' she said.

Sid raised an eyebrow. 'Does this mean you've solved the last part of the puzzle?'

'It seems to be painful, but he can stand up and walk if he really needs to.'

'So simple,' Sid nodded.

'PG just sent this picture to Monika,' she said, handing him her phone.

'He was drinking pretty heavily earlier,' Sid mumbled, enlarging the image.

'What do you see?'

'Desperation, possibly guilt. A cry for help.'

They turned and went back over to the bar. André had moved the carafe of whisky and taken out a sticky bottle of chartreuse, which he was busy pouring into a clean shaker. Björn set down his empty glass on the edge of the counter and used his fingertips to push it back.

'What picture are you talking about?' he asked.

'PG's current status,' said Julia, holding up her phone for him to see.

Björn burped into his clenched fist. 'Looks like my place a few hours from now ... Except for the iron key,' he said, pointing to his glass as André started pouring the liqueur and crushed ice.

'Do you know what it's for?' Julia asked.

'The iron key,' he repeated, his eyes lingering on her.

Julia enlarged the image as far as she could and studied the old key, which was half hidden beneath the pack of pills. It looked to be almost twenty centimetres long, with a length of red yarn threaded through the head.

'Which door is it for?' she asked, heart racing.

'Ask André. I'm not trusted to handle it,' said Björn, setting his glass down on a coaster.

'It's for the brewhouse,' said André.

'My brother looks after the key because he's afraid I'll go over there and knock the cabinets over or tear down the chandeliers when I'm wasted.'

'I'm afraid you'll hurt yourself,' André corrected him.

'Was the brewhouse typically kept locked?' she asked.

'Always,' said Björn.

'And who has a key?'

'Just me and PG,' said André.

'Where is yours?'

'Back at my place. On Lars Norén's old keyring. I won it at auction, paid a fortune for it. Just so you know, in case you feel the urge to wreck anything else.'

'Could anyone have taken your key?' she asked.

'I mean, I suppose it's possible, but I tend to keep the door locked.'

'Does Björn have a key to your place?'

'Nope.'

'So who does?'

'No one except Amelie. She helps me with the washing and cleaning.'

'Was the brewhouse unlocked on the day of the AGM?'

'It's never unlocked,' Björn said with a repressed smile.

Julia turned away and crossed the creaking floor to the large window, leaning on her cane as she looked outside. She had been too rash, and she had made a huge mistake.

'Julia? What's going on?'

'I was in too much of a hurry again,' she said, failing to keep her voice calm.

'What do you mean?'

Julia left him by the window, making her way through the grand rooms as quickly as she could.

Björn hadn't had access to the scene of the murder. Some of the other outhouses might have been left open, but since the brewhouse was used to store valuable antiques, they made sure the door was always locked.

Sid caught up with her by the foot of the stairs in the entrance hall. Julia had tears in her eyes as she turned to him.

'It wasn't Björn,' she said, gritting her teeth.

'You can't keep doing this, Julia.'

'I know.'

'I don't understand. You need to ... You need to talk to me, not just act on impulse. I don't understand why you wanted me to come if you—'

'Go home, then!' she cut him off. 'I'll get the train back once I'm done.'

'Is that what you want?'

'Yes.'

'Christ, I knew this was a mistake,' he said, his voice hard.

'Sorry,' she mumbled, looking up and meeting his eye.

'You and I don't work well together, we never have ...'

'Don't say that,' she said, feeling her chin start to tremble.

'Christ, Julia.'

'I thought I was right ... I'm sorry.'

She turned away, moved over to the door and stepped out into the cool air to wait for the police.

She would have to explain that it was all just a mistake and apologise profusely.

The hairs on her arms stood on end as she saw the first flash of headlights coming down the avenue of trees.

The light swung between the trees on both sides of the car like the oars of a Viking longboat.

Julia made her way down towards the turning circle, pausing on the bottom step and leaning against her cane.

The car pulled up in front of her on the gravel, the blue lights on its roof dark.

# 34

Julia had tears in her eyes as the taxi took her away from the manor house at high speed. She was in the back seat, still wearing her sleek evening gown with bare shoulders and an open back.

The two police officers – a tall woman with a blonde ponytail and an older man with crooked shoulders – had listened to her excuses, told her to stay where she was and then gone inside to talk to Monika and the others. When they came back out, they had given Julia a dressing-down. There was nothing she could say, and so she simply stood there and took it with downcast eyes. She then apologised again and called for a cab the minute the patrol car had disappeared down the avenue.

She couldn't face the others right now.

Sid would be embarrassed on her behalf.

Why did she always have to make these mistakes?

It was unbearable at times.

Julia closed her eyes.

From the car radio, she could hear a woman singing about wanting to get high on a beach in a melancholic, almost laconic voice.

It was eleven thirty when the cab pulled up outside the Royal Club in central Sundsvall. Julia paid, grabbed her cane and then got out of the car.

In her thin silk dress, she immediately felt cold.

A tall woman in an extravagant tuxedo was smoking outside the club, tapping her ash into a whisky bottle full of water by the wall.

Julia made her way past her, nodded to the bouncer and entered the old cinema building. She could hear music pulsing from the room next door.

A thin woman with a grey face was leaning against the wall by the toilets. Her mascara had run down her cheeks, and her pink fur bolero was on the floor by her feet. She was breathing heavily, as though she was about to have a panic attack, and her friend was doing her best to calm her down, a hand on her chest.

Up ahead, there were a number of flags. Trans flags, pride flags, queer flags and others Julia didn't recognise.

A crowd of people had gathered in front of an enormous mirror with a gold Baroque frame and were using it to fix their make-up. Most of them were dressed up, glittery and tasteful, and Julia heard them complimenting one another and laughing.

She walked through a cloud of hairspray towards a set of swinging doors, using her cane to push it open and make her way through to the dance floor on the other side.

Club music thundered from the speakers, the bass so loud she could feel it pulsing through her body. Overhead, the colourful lights flashed rhythmically. Around twenty people were standing by the stage, roughly the same number over by the bar. In the middle of the platform, a drag king with pale skin, a neat beard and a tall top hat was dancing.

Julia paused, overcome by just how badly she had failed once again. She had let Sidney down, and now he was angry, regretted ever agreeing to work alongside her.

It was a good job she hadn't had time to mention her proposal yet, she thought.

She sighed deeply, tried to force back her anxiety and told herself that she gave too much credit to Sid. It wasn't true that he was the only person she could stand to have touch her, as though he possessed some sort of magic. He was just an ordinary man she had happened to fall in love with, a man she had also betrayed because her head was such a mess.

She needed to give him up and find someone else to project all her pathetic hopes and needs onto.

Julia started making her way across the dance floor, taking a snaking route to avoid bumping into anyone.

In the raised booth, she could see a muscular DJ with a buzz cut, tattooed arms and full breasts. Her shadow swayed back and forth on the filthy plexiglass screen.

Julia stepped on an empty plastic glass, which shattered beneath her foot.

Up ahead, a woman in black was trying to catch her eye, but Julia turned off to one side, holding her back with her cane when the woman approached.

The dancer on the stage was wearing an open jacket over a silver vest, tight silver hot pants and heavy black boots. He seemed to be approaching some sort of finale, thrusting his hips.

A few young women in front of the stage were filming him on their phones, screaming with excitement. They grabbed some knickers from a glittery bucket and threw them onto the stage.

A golden streamer had caught on Julia's heel, and the slit in her dress gaped open as she bent down to dislodge it using her cane.

The music died down, and the audience clapped and whistled. The dancer sniffed his armpit, bowed and then made way for a new king – a man with a huge belly, a hairy chest and tattooed shoulders.

Julia had reached the bar, and she ordered a bottle of IPA, took a swig and then turned to the dancer, who had just come down from the stage.

'I only caught the end of your number, but it was incredible,' said Julia.

'Thanks,' Frida replied with a laugh, lowering her top hat to the bar.

'You never answer the phone.'

'I do, just not very often.'

'There's something I need to talk to you about,' Julia explained.

'OK, but it'll have to be quick – I need to get changed before I go on again.'

'It's about André.'

'This is actually where we met. He spent all evening trying to come onto me before he finally got it, but we became friends after that.'

'You said he was at your place at three o'clock on Sunday.'

'We had a coffee,' Frida confirmed.

'And you're sure of the time?'

'Yup.'

'So he closed the shop just for a coffee?'

'He had to be at Mannheim for five anyway, and he needed to get something out of my safe,' Frida explained, waving to the bartender.

'What did he have in there?'

'I don't know. An envelope, I think. He keeps some stuff at my place.'

'He didn't mention what it was?'

'He was just stressed about having to spend time with the family.'

A short drag king in a tight white sailor's uniform tugged on Frida's arm and whispered something in her ear.

'My friend here wants an introduction,' said Frida. 'This is Querelle, from Timrå.'

'Hi,' said Julia, clinking bottles with him before she took another swig of beer.

'You're the most beautiful woman I've ever seen,' said Querelle, pushing his hat back.

'He's a bit drunk,' Frida explained with a grin.

'I love the cane and the sexy scar,' he continued, moving a step closer. 'I want to trace it with my tongue and ...'

He stopped talking as Julia took a step back, and his outstretched hand dropped to his side.

'Sorry,' Julia mumbled.

'None of this is infectious, you know,' said Frida.

'I know, I know, it's just that I'm damaged ... In here, I mean,' she said, pointing to her head.

'It's OK,' said Querelle.

'No, it's not, but it's not what you think. I'd love to get you a drink and just—'

'No need,' he cut her off.

'Wait, give me a chance,' she said. 'What would you like?'

'I'm fine, thanks.'

'Come on, have a drink.'

'OK, fine. Same as you, then,' he said with a sceptical smile. 'Frida?'

'I don't have time, sorry. I need to go and get changed,' she said, hurrying away.

Julia ordered another two beers, and she and Querelle sat down at the end of the bar. They clinked bottles and drank. Behind them, the crowd had started clapping, and the fragmented light from a disco ball danced across the walls.

'So... I have a pretty serious form of PTSD,' Julia explained, taking a deep breath. 'Which, among other things, makes all forms of physical contact incredibly difficult for me. I can't really explain it, but that's the reason. Just so you know.'

'What happened?' asked Querelle.

'What do you mean?'

'Where does the trauma stem from?'

'I lost my entire family when I was thirteen... A plane crash,' she replied, swallowing hard.

'God.'

'Mum, Dad, and my two little sisters. I can't say their names or I'll—'

'Here, take this,' said Querelle, handing her a napkin.

'Uff, here I am crying anyway,' Julia said, attempting to smile.

'Good.'

She dried her cheeks and thought about the fact that she had never come out and said any of that before, not even with her therapist or Sid. They knew, of course, but she had never explicitly told them. Julia couldn't quite believe that she had just spoken about the disaster with a complete stranger in a bar.

'Three hundred and seventy-two people died that day,' she continued. 'I was the only survivor, and I have no idea why. I've spent so long searching for answers, but I just can't understand it. There aren't any answers. All I can do is live with the guilt and ... the feeling of lying among severed body parts ... slowly growing colder and ...'

She trailed off and looked into Querelle's pretty eyes for a moment before turning to the stage. A new drag king in leather and studs was playing a ukulele covered in skulls.

'I don't believe there are any answers either,' said Querelle.

'No,' said Julia, looking at him again.

'I'm not religious,' he continued, 'but whenever things feel tough I like to tell myself that before any of us are picked to be born, we're visited by a god or an angel who says: "I've got a deal, if you're interested. I'll give you the spark of life and you'll exist for a short time. You'll experience all sorts of grief, pain, anxiety and loneliness ... and you're also guaranteed to die."'

'That's just it.'

'And everyone offered that deal shouts, "Yes! I accept those terms, of course I do!" Because that's how incredible life is. How big.'

Julia nodded. She wished Querelle would give her a hug, she realised, but she couldn't quite bring herself to say it.

Up on the stage, the dancer had torn off his leather trousers, and pretended not to have noticed that his big rubber penis was hanging out the side of his underpants.

# 35

THE CHAPEL WHERE THE FUNERAL would take place was like a small flash of red by the edge of the trees just downstream of the old mill.

PG had got his way, and the pathologist had released Werther's body that morning.

At the bar last night, Julia had finished her beer, thanked Querelle for being such a great listener and then taken a cab back to Mannheim filled with an odd sense of calm. By the time she woke, however, that feeling was gone. Instead, she was full of regret over the way she had accused Björn and her meeting with the police officers, but she refused to be ashamed of her conversation in the bar.

Julia had decided not to go down to breakfast, and had been in her room all morning. She had ignored Sid when he knocked, refused to answer any calls and hadn't read any text messages. But he had now caught up with her on the path to the chapel, and was walking alongside her in silence. Butterflies danced weightlessly over the nettles and bird vetch.

'I thought you were going home,' she said after a moment or two.

'Yeah, but I changed my mind when I realised that was just your way of trying to get out of paying me,' he joked.

'Shit . . . I really thought you'd fall for it,' she replied with a smile, a wave of relief starting to rise up inside her.

Julia caught a tall stem of grass between her fingers and snapped off the seed head as they kept walking.

'You disappeared yesterday,' said Sid.

'I just needed to get away for a while,' she explained, letting the seeds scatter to the ground.

'OK.'

'I don't know. I was upset and ashamed . . . about everything,' she said. 'I'm so, so sick of myself, and I know I rush things sometimes. It's like I just can't help myself once I get going.'

'It's OK,' he said.

'No, it's not. I embarrassed you, and I'm sorry.'

'You'll find the key soon.'

'Do you really think so?'

A thick plank of wood had been laid as a kind of bridge over a patch of mud, and it squelched softly under their weight.

'There's something I didn't get round to telling you about the film of the King,' said Sid. 'You remember Sylvester's wife Linnea at the very beginning?'

'Yes, she was so beautiful.'

'Did you notice her ring? She was wearing a diamond ring on her left hand. It looked like the same one Siri wears now. I just thought you should know.'

'Are you sure?'

'No, but it was a pretty big diamond,' he said. 'Old European-cut, from before the more modern techniques gained popularity. They don't glitter the same way. They've got a ... how can I put it? ... different kind of sheen. That technique fell out of fashion around 1930, and the setting also had an Art-Deco feel to it—'

'OK, Sid, I get it,' she cut him off. 'You think it's the same ring.'

'Was I being boring again?'

'No,' she replied with a smile.

'You thought so.'

A small stream babbled in the middle of the dry riverbed by the side of the path.

'How do you know so much about rings, anyway?' asked Julia.

'I proposed to someone once,' he replied, taking her hand.

Back when they were married, they had lived on the top floor of a handsome turn-of-the-century building on Roslagsgatan in Stockholm. From the arched windows of the living room, they had been able to see the treetops in Haga Park in the distance. On the other side of the hall to their bedroom, there had been a small room with a sloping ceiling, a dormer window and yellow tempera walls.

Julia couldn't bring herself to enjoy the moment, walking hand in hand like they always had. The sense of failure was too powerful. Her throat was still aching with repressed tears, and as they approached the others she tried to calm herself and adopt a neutral expression.

Her cane sent a few pebbles tumbling down into the water, and a shimmering green dragonfly darted away along the bank.

Sid let go of her hand and held back a leafy branch that was hanging low over the path.

As they approached the chapel, they overheard Monika and Siri bickering.

'Couldn't you find a shorter skirt?' Monika snapped.

'Yeah, but then everyone would've been able to see that I'm not wearing any fucking knickers.'

The two women fell silent when they spotted Sid and Julia. Siri attempted to smile, but her eyes were joyless. She was wearing a pleated black skirt and a short jacket.

Monika seemed furious, her cheeks flushed. She was wearing a black velvet coat, and her hair was slicked back.

'The police rang,' she said, fixing her eyes on Julia. 'They've called PG in for an interview.'

'Is he a suspect?' she asked.

'I don't think so, no.'

Julia made her way over to PG, who was leaning back against the wall of the chapel. His furrowed face was grey, and he was wearing a long black coat, a dark suit and a white tie.

'You sent another photograph yesterday,' she told him.

He looked up at her with bloodshot eyes. 'Yes, Monika mentioned it, but I'm afraid I don't remember much.'

'What do you remember?'

'From yesterday?' He rubbed his face. 'God,' he mumbled. 'The lawyer, she told us that Siri had inherited everything ...'

'But the meeting with the lawyer was at 4 p.m. What happened after that?'

'I'm not sure ... Did we eat dinner together?'

'No, but we met later, for cocktails. You were playing records on the old gramophone, you danced with Monika.'

He stared blankly at her. 'I'm sorry, I don't remember any of that ...'

The grey clouds parted briefly, allowing the sunlight to spill down onto the forest and the water.

Sid and Julia waited until the family had filed into the chapel before following them in. They had lit candles inside, and the coffin had been placed in front of the simple altar. A wreath of white roses with a ribbon reading "Beloved – Missed" lay on the floor to one side.

André was already sitting at the front of the hall, Björn in his wheelchair in the aisle beside him.

The sound of chatter and scraping feet bounced between the walls as everyone took their seats.

A few minutes later, the vicar emerged from the sacristy. She had shiny glasses and grey hair, gathered in a plaited bun at the nape of her neck.

Julia's heart began to race.

The disaster that stole her family from her had, once more, been locked away with her unforgivable betrayal of Sidney.

The truth was unbearable in both cases.

In order to make it through the ceremony, she focused everything she had on the imaginary photograph from her own family's funeral, taken from the vaulted ceiling of the cathedral.

At the top edge of the image, she could see the lower section of the cross, Jesus's bloody toes. And down below: four white coffins on the stone floor.

A lone girl in a dress sat in the front row, listening to music through headphones with a white cable.

Julia only returned to reality when the vicar asked them to all stand.

No one sang along with the hymn, and once the vicar stopped speaking, PG slowly made his way over to the coffin and patted the lid.

'Goodbye, big brother,' he said.

\* \* \*

By the time they left the chapel, the wind had picked up. It shook the tall pines, making it sound as though there was a raging sea somewhere nearby. Monika thanked the vicar for a beautiful ceremony and then tied a black shawl around her head.

'We've prepared a simple buffet back at Mannheim, if you'd like to join us,' she said.

'Thank you, but I'm afraid I have to get back to Sundsvall. I'm just going to turn out the lights and tidy up before I leave,' the vicar replied, squeezing Monika's hands before she walked away.

André's wavy hair blew across his face as he wheeled his brother outside. Björn was sitting with his head bowed, his mouth downturned and his eyes puffy. André pushed him over to the rented car and tried to lift him into the backseat.

'Hold on, let me help you,' said Monika, hurrying over.

One of Björn's feet had caught on the footrest, and the whole chair was on the verge of tipping as André tried to pull him free.

'I'm freezing, I'm going to head back,' said Siri, turning and setting off in the direction of the house.

Julia caught Sid's eye, and he immediately understood what she wanted.

'Shall I keep you company?' he asked.

Siri paused and turned around. She seemed surprised, but then she smiled and nodded.

Once Björn was safely in the backseat, André folded the wheelchair and loaded it into the boot.

'I'll join you in the car,' said Monika, opening the door and getting into the passenger seat.

'Of course,' PG mumbled.

There was a loud crack as the car rolled over a dry twig, swung around and pulled away.

Julia was now alone with PG, exactly as she had hoped.

'Where do you keep your iron key?' she asked, fixing her eyes on him.

'It's always on me,' he said, patting his coat pocket.

'Tell me about it.'

PG took out the key and held it up on its red string, enabling her to take it from him without accidentally touching his hand.

'It's a symbol of tradition, of inheritance and responsibility...'

'Nice,' she said with a smile, weighing it in her hand.

Julia studied the key in the dappled sunlight filtering through the swaying branches.

Decades of use had worn the metal smooth in places, and it shimmered like silver thread alongside the dull rust.

'Mannheim gave each of his sons one key. They were master keys that could be used to open any door, but now that the brewhouse is gone they no longer open anything.'

'We'll see about that,' Julia mumbled.

# 36

Julia returned the key to PG, and they slowly started walking back towards the manor house. The dry needles and pine cones crunched underfoot.

'Is it true that André has the other key?' she asked.

'Strictly speaking, it should be Björn – he's the eldest – but that would never work,' said PG. 'Just as I took care of Werther's when he left Mannheim.'

'Do you know what André keeps in his girlfriend's safe?'

'No idea.'

'Did he bring anything to the meeting? An envelope, a document?'

'No, nothing.'

They continued in silence. Siri and Sid were much faster, and were no longer in view up ahead.

'Why exactly did Werther leave Mannheim? Why did he become a recluse?' asked Julia.

'I think our childhood probably did him more harm than it did me. I was too young to really understand everything.'

'You weren't damaged by it, you mean?'

'It's hard to think of one's self in those terms, but you're probably right. Everything leaves a mark.'

Julia saw PG shudder, and she realised that the marks he was talking about were deep in his soul.

'I understand that your mother took her own life,' she said.

'Yes,' he whispered, his eyes on the ground.

'I'm sorry about the timing, but I have to ask. We've almost completed our investigation, and I'm planning on heading home this evening.'

'Oh, wow,' he said, pausing. 'So can you tell me whether I'm guilty? Am I? Did I kill my own brother?'

'It's still a bit too early to say.'

'I'd like a full report, of course. Discreetly, so I can tell Monika what you've concluded in my own way . . . I know her, you see; she can get rather anxious.'

'Our confidentiality clause still applies . . . but if I can find the answers to a few outstanding questions then I plan to go over everything in the library. It's up to you who is there for that.'

They started walking again.

'Who do you think should be there?' he asked after a moment or two.

'It's probably best if everyone is. They'll find out the truth at some point anyway, once the legal process gets underway.'

'OK, then that's what we'll do . . . even though it makes me nervous just thinking about it.'

A blackbird cut across the sky in a perfect arc.

'Why did your mother end her life?' Julia asked.

PG quietly cleared his throat, reaching up to touch his mouth. Julia knew he was about to tell her something important, so she held her tongue.

'Our mother had an affair, one that threatened to become a scandal,' he said. 'She made one mistake, but the accusations just wouldn't stop, the suspicions ... And so she found a way to put an end to the gossip.'

'Who was this relationship with?'

'It wasn't a relationship, as such. She was caught in bed with her husband's cousin, with Augustus.'

'Björn, André and Siri's father?'

PG nodded.

'How did that come to light? Do you know?'

They paused again, and Julia leaned against her cane as she studied him.

'Yes, I do ... My father told me, years after my mother passed. He'd been to a dinner with some of the other forest owners, away from home for the first time in two months. And when he got back, he saw his cousin's car outside. That made him suspicious, so he marched inside and grabbed the gun from the Red Room, shot the chandelier to pieces and then stormed up the stairs, where he found them both in the hallway. The door to their bedroom was open, and my mother was half naked, her hair a mess ... His cousin stumbled forward with his shoes in his hands, jacket draped over his arm. My father said he would have shot them both right there and then if it hadn't been for Werther getting in the way ...'

PG's voice broke, and they moved on again in silence.

Julia noticed that Sid and Siri had paused by the dam. She and PG would catch up with them before long.

'So you think your mother killed herself to put an end to the gossip?' she said.

'Anyone can make a mistake ... I mean, just look at me. But ...' He trailed off, as though he regretted his words.

'What were you going to say?'

'It isn't fair, the yardsticks differ, but some mistakes simply cling to a person. And my mother's misstep could have ruined the family name, damaged the business.'

'That sounds like a rather old-fashioned way of looking at things.'

'Yes, but I think she did the right thing. I'd do the same if the family's honour was on the line. I mean, my father was the majority owner and managing director, he couldn't have a wife who ... well, I'm sure you can imagine the talk. It just couldn't happen.'

'Do you remember all this?' Julia asked, her interest piqued. 'What it was like? The period leading up to her suicide?'

'Not really, I just remember my father acting oddly, that we were sent to stay with relatives in Umeå for a while. I don't know, I was only eight. All I really remember is that my mother kept crying when we got back, two days before she died. I was walking down the hallway upstairs, and I got frightened when I heard her, she sounded so quiet and despairing ... I'd never heard anything like it before.'

They had reached the dam. The police cordon was gone, but the ground where Werther's body had briefly lain was muddy and covered in tyre tracks. A few small plastic bags from the crime scene technicians were still floating in the water.

Sid turned around and fixed his eyes on Julia and PG.

'What were you talking about?' Julia asked.

'Werther being gone, how I just can't believe it,' Siri whispered, turning and continuing towards the manor house.

'We'll have a little memorial when we get home,' said PG, setting off after her.

Julia watched the two Motts, walking along the same path some ten metres apart. The youngest member of the family, followed by the eldest.

'Whoever killed Werther must have known that his body would float up to the surface at the dam,' said Sid. 'It would have been far better just to drag him into the woods and bury him there, or at least tie him to something heavy before they threw him in.'

# 37

THE MEMORIAL IN THE DRAWING room began with a speech about Werther's good sides – a speech that, for obvious reasons, would be rather short, as PG explained when he tapped his glass and got to his feet.

'But I do remember one occasion when he built me an igloo,' he continued. 'It was so beautiful, with windows made from thin sheets of ice. We filled it with blankets, and we drank hot chocolate, read *Tintin* ... I know what you're thinking, that doesn't sound like Werther, but before our mother died he could actually be nice sometimes.'

Once PG's speech was over, they drank champagne and turned to the buffet: oysters on an enormous bed of ice, Provençal beef, potato salad, chocolate cake, cheeses and grapes. The atmosphere quickly became merry, almost bizarrely so.

PG loosened his tie and made his way around the group with a magnum of champagne, filling their coupé glasses. Björn's face was relaxed, and André came in with traces of white powder clinging to the stubble beneath his nose, laughing hysterically at something. His dark hair was now slicked back again, but he had taken off his jacket and rolled up his shirtsleeves.

The ice cubes rattled in the bucket as Monika took out another magnum and let it drip for a few seconds before removing the foil. The cork popped loudly, making Siri shriek. Björn clapped his hands.

Amelie came in with a tray and began clearing away the dirty plates, but Monika made her stop and thrust a glass of champagne into her hand.

Björn put down his glass and rolled slowly over to the door.

Sid took out his phone, glanced down at it, then met Julia's eye and nodded.

Julia lowered her cutlery, grabbed her cane and set off after Björn.

She waited a few metres from the door while he went into the toilet. After a few minutes, she heard the flush, the taps running, and then he re-emerged.

'Fair warning, there might be a bit of piss on the seat,' he said.

'I need to talk to you.'

'Why, you called the cops on me again?'

'I was wrong, and I'm sorry about that. I really am.'

He sighed and drummed his fingers on the armrest of his chair. 'It's fine ... You called my bluff, what can I say?'

Julia knew this was where she should ask him about blackmail, about the shares Werther had transferred to him, but instead she decided to try to catch him off guard.

'Your mother Cecilia went through periods of deep depression. Do you remember when that started?'

A look of genuine surprise flickered over his face. 'Yes, more or less ...'

'Siri thought your mother suffered from postnatal depression after giving birth to her.'

'I don't,' he said quietly.

'No? What do you think?'

It was clear he found the conversation uncomfortable. His cynical smile was gone, and he looked like all he wanted was to get away.

'Does it matter?'

'Did her depression stem from the fact that your father had an affair with his cousin's wife?'

'I guess so ...'

'You knew about that?'

'It tore the family apart, that affair. They had so many fucking arguments, Dad started drinking ... Screaming at her that he hadn't done anything wrong.'

'What did you make of that?'

'I once told Werther that his mother was a whore. I knew he'd give me a beating for it, and he did hit me, but only the once. He said it was all a lie, that the only thing that happened that evening was that he'd called my dad because he was scared of the dark. Sylvester wouldn't be home until late, and both PG and Linnea were sleeping ... Werther said that he and my old man were playing cards in his room when they heard the gunshot. Sylvester had come home blind drunk and shot the ceiling to shit ...'

'So you don't think they were having an affair after all?'

'What does that matter now?'

Julia watched as he rolled off towards the drawing room, and she felt the pressure of her feet on the floor lightening, eventually disappearing entirely.

In her mind's eye, she fired the gun and saw broken glass raining down from the ceiling, Bohemian crystal shattering on contact with the parquet floor as she staggered out of the study, past the grand piano in the drawing room and into the entrance hall.

She took a deep breath and felt her full weight again, the pain in her leg. She ran through the steps one last time, then made her way back through to the others.

Django Reinhardt's rhythmic jazz guitar was playing over the speakers. Björn had torn a napkin to shreds and threw the pieces up into the air above Amelie, making them rain down on her like confetti.

PG and Monika were standing by the bar. She lit a cigarette and took a drag, coughing softly. He reached around and put a hand on her bottom, whispering something with a smile.

André held up a bottle to the light as he chatted to Siri. His crisp shirt had a half-moon sweat stain on the back. Siri used the lid of her red lipstick as a mirror to apply a fresh coat to her lips.

Julia moved over to Sid, thanking him when he passed back her champagne glass.

'I'm looking forward to dinner with you,' she whispered.

'Of course you are,' he replied.

She raised her glass to her lips, took a thoughtful sip and then grabbed a spoon from a dessert bowl and used it to get everyone's attention.

'Hello, everyone,' she said. 'It's been incredibly informative and interesting to spend a few days with you here. Sid and I have now completed our investigation, and I'd like to share our conclusions. I suggest we all make our way through to the Red Room.'

# 38

Someone had switched off the music, but the mood was still surprisingly cheery as they made their way into the Red Room clutching their bottles, plates and glasses. The gravity of the moment probably hadn't quite had time to sink in yet, thought Julia; most of the Motts seemed to think the situation was simply a little absurd.

Sid and Amelie set out the chairs in a line, and the murmuring, giggling family took their seats.

'You want me to sit down too?' a surprised Amelie asked when Sid gestured for her to do the same.

'Yes, of course!' PG shouted, pouring her a top up.

Siri lowered her plate to her lap and exchanged an amused look with Julia.

Monika was radiating a sense of controlled calm, smoothing out her skirt with a smile as she sat down.

Afternoon had begun to give way to evening, and the forest on the other side of the colourful windows seemed to be bathed in a mosaic of greenish-black hues.

The portraits of the firstborn sons gazed down at the small group, who stopped speaking and grew serious as Julia crossed the floor and stood in front of them.

'From the moment we arrived here, we have been putting the pieces of a puzzle together,' she said. 'It was much more complex than we first thought, but I think we now have everything in place.'

Her eyes scanned the group, lingering on every face before she next spoke. 'On Sunday, at three in the afternoon, Werther Mott was killed in the brewhouse by the dam.'

'The cause of death was a heavy blow to the head, with what we believe was probably some sort of short-handled hammer – a so-called club hammer,' said Sid.

PG shifted uncomfortably in his chair, and André leaned in to Björn and whispered something in his ear.

'The person who killed Werther Mott is in this room,' Julia continued.

'This is all so surreal,' Monika mumbled, sounding stressed.

Julia waited until all eyes were on her again, clearing her throat before she went on.

'We've reached the point where I need to ask whether you'd like a clean, sanitised version of the truth, or the full truth – in all its brutal clarity,' she said.

'What's the point if we don't get to hear everything?' asked Björn.

'So you want the whole truth?' she repeated.

'Yes, yes, of course,' PG muttered.

A compact silence immediately settled over the room. No one was smiling now. Everyone seemed to be dreading whatever was about to be revealed.

Siri was staring up at Julia with wide eyes, and Monika was fiddling with her wedding ring. Amelie's face was in shadow, sitting as still as a statue.

'Does everyone agree?' Julia asked.

'Yes,' André replied, sounding bored.

'Good, then I'd like to start with Björn, who doesn't have an alibi for the time of the murder. And who has also hated Werther since he was a child.'

'Everyone hated Werther,' Björn spoke up in a raspy voice.

'That's true, but he caused you serious harm as an adult. And your hatred of him continued even after he transferred a ten per cent stake in the company to you, possibly more to avoid a scandal as a result of a legal battle, by the sounds of it.'

'I don't know, it was André who negotiated with him,' said Björn, turning to his brother.

'Ten per cent is a lot, but I still sensed a slight humiliation on your part, at having been paid to keep quiet.'

'I don't give a shit about that,' he said.

'During our first conversations with each of you, Björn was the only person who revealed that he knew Werther was planning to come to the shareholders' meeting,' Julia continued. 'And he also correctly assumed that Werther had been beaten to death.'

A murmur passed through the room.

'I imagined Björn arranging a meeting with Werther. Who knows, maybe he was drunk and wanted to get his own back, once and for all? We now know that Werther took a taxi straight from the station to the brewhouse, where he was killed almost immediately ... Subjected to "blunt force trauma," as Sid said.'

'The hammer used to kill Werther was likely one of Björn's tools, and was later also destroyed in the fire,' said Sid.

Amelie put down her glass, and PG rubbed his mouth.

Julia paused to take a sip of water. The evening sun had disappeared behind a bank of cloud, and the indirect darkness had caused the shadows to deepen like folds in material.

'Certain aspects of this scenario seemed implausible until I discovered that Björn can still walk if he needs to – even if he does find it hard, painful... He was certainly capable of getting up from his wheelchair and taking PG's phone from the dresser in the service corridor,' Julia continued.

'You goddamn fraud,' PG said with an astounded smile.

'What is this?' asked Monika.

'Just wait,' Julia reassured her. 'I was convinced I'd found our killer – I even called the police – but I had missed one key piece of the puzzle: the iron key. The brewhouse was kept locked, and Björn didn't have access to the key. I apologise, Björn.'

'Fucking bitch,' André muttered.

'This is just the top of the shit mountain,' said Björn.

'I was also wrong to assume that Björn's injuries and the fact that he now has to use a wheelchair were the reason Werther transferred ten per cent to him, but let's put a pin in that for a moment.'

'What's she talking about?' asked André, looking around at the others with his usual smile.

'I just wanted to start by admitting to my mistakes. Björn had the means and the motive, and he also had no alibi, but he didn't kill Werther. Which takes us to Per Günter Mott, who hired us to look into this in the first place. Is he the killer?'

PG held out his hands in an exaggerated shrug.

'A lot of the circumstantial evidence points to him, there's no denying that,' Julia continued. 'The photograph was on his phone, which he claims to have left on the dresser, though no one can confirm that. He lacks an alibi for the time of the murder, and was also seen coming back up the road from the brewhouse just a few minutes after the picture was taken. He has a history of drinking too much, of gaps in his memory and of taking pictures in compromising situations. PG also had a complicated relationship with his brother, and was often humiliated by him . . . And let's not forget that no one but the lawyer knew about Werther's will. PG must have thought he stood to inherit Werther's share of the estate if he died, which is a powerful motive.'

'I agree,' said PG, as much to himself as anything.

'He came to my office in Stockholm to find out the truth after what he claimed was a near-complete gap in his memory from the day of the meeting. He started drinking at breakfast, took fifty milligrams of anti-anxiety medication before lunch – a medication that also happens to have a tranquilising effect, particularly in combination with alcohol – and was completely out of it after dinner. PG has accounted for fragments of that day, which fits with the way amnesia of this type works, but it still seemed odd that he wouldn't remember *anything* of the murder itself, which took place at three o'clock.'

'Yes,' Monika mumbled.

'But PG's desire to get to the bottom of whether he was guilty or not before turning to the police seemed genuine to me.'

'I still don't know whether I did it,' said PG, his eyes welling up.

'Björn was the only one who claimed to know that Werther was planning to attend the meeting, but the truth is that PG had received an email in which his older brother set out his plans to come and vote in favour of selling Mannheim – which would have seemed like a disaster to PG.'

'I didn't know that,' he said with a frown.

'No, because the message ended up in his junk mail folder. Still, PG had the key to the brewhouse, and could easily have arranged to meet Werther and then killed him there. But he didn't do any of these things.'

PG stared up at her and Sid. 'Are you sure?'

'You didn't kill your brother.'

His face flushed in relief. 'Oh, thank God.'

# 39

Julia's eyes swept over them all, pausing on Amelie, who was slumped in her seat. As ever, she was wearing a nondescript black dress and a white apron. Her bare face was pale, the tip of her nose red.

'Amelie ... You had the opportunity to take André's iron key during the shareholders' meeting,' Julia began with renewed energy.

'I didn't do it,' she stuttered.

'Amelie has an alibi for the time when the photograph was taken, but not for the murder,' Julia continued.

'OK ... ?' PG mumbled.

'As you all know, Amelie always requests time off whenever Werther comes to visit. We haven't gone into any real detail about what happened in the kitchen six years ago, but it's clear it was a case of serious sexual harassment – possibly even attempted rape. Werther came in and Amelie defended herself with a knife, badly injuring him, whether intentionally or not. Werther ended up needing sixteen stitches on his abdomen.'

'We never asked any questions,' Monika said quietly. 'But we all knew it must be something along those lines.'

'Don't you find it odd that you never asked any questions? As Amelie's employer? As a fellow woman?' Julia went on. 'Amelie has been in your lives for the past thirty years; you see her practically every day.'

'I'm sorry, Amelie,' said Monika.

'One could conceivably imagine Amelie finding out that Werther was coming to the meeting – possibly from Björn – too late for her to find a replacement, and so she arranged to meet him in the brewhouse to talk plainly. Or simply to finish what she started in the kitchen.'

The atmosphere was now so tense that everyone flinched when Siri accidentally dropped her fork to the floor.

'Sorry,' she whispered, bending down to retrieve it.

'But she didn't. Amelie didn't kill Werther,' said Julia.

Amelie looked up and smiled.

'She has only ever tried to do her job here, forced to negotiate a far-from-simple working environment. Amelie isn't involved in any form of criminality – unlike André.'

'What, so I'm the one who did it now, am I?' he snapped with an irritable smile.

'Your girlfriend Frida is loyal, but she hasn't been able to confirm that André went over to her apartment before midnight on the Sunday in question. But—'

'So I got the detail wrong, that's not a crime.'

'But he keeps one—'

'You know what *is* a crime? Smashing up someone's car.'

'He keeps one of the iron keys at home, and he most likely also knew that Werther was planning to attend the meeting, because he'd seen Björn the day before.'

'Seriously, would you just give up?' said André, waving dismissively.

His forehead was now slick with sweat.

'We assumed the ten per cent was compensation for Björn's injuries, but that whole charade actually had nothing to do with Werther's shares. No, it's a simple case of insurance fraud. The reason Werther handed over his shares was because André was blackmailing him. I did wonder if André and Werther might have agreed to meet prior to the meeting, in order to negotiate, and something went wrong.'

Julia took a few steps towards André, raised her cane and pressed the tip to his chest.

'Are you waiting for me to confess to something?' he asked, calmly swatting it away.

'I'll get to that,' Julia replied. 'But before we move on, I'd like to straighten out a few things from the past ... As you all know, there are two branches of the family. You have the same great grandfather, Mannheim Mott, who was responsible for building the empire. PG, your grandfather Leopold was Mannheim's eldest son, which meant he inherited everything. He had one son, your father Sylvester, and Sylvester and his wife Linnea had two sons, Per Günter and Werther.'

'We know all this,' André sighed.

'Björn, André and Siri, your grandfather inherited nothing but the two houses by the river. He had a son and two daughters. His son Augustus, your father, inherited the houses, but other than that he came away empty-handed – at least until PG's father transferred thirty per cent of the entire company to him. This hushed-up episode seems to suggest that—'

'Come on, then. Out with the dirty laundry,' said André. 'Hang it out for everyone to—'

Julia brought her cane down on the table, and he immediately stopped talking.

'It seems to suggest that Augustus,' she continued, her voice louder this time, 'had a sexual relationship with your mother, PG – something that threatened to become a scandal. I was convinced that the transfer of the thirty per cent had to be a case of blackmail—'

'The apple doesn't fall far from the tree,' Monika mumbled.

'But would Sylvester really give his cousin Augustus thirty per cent just to avoid a scandal?' Julia mused.

'The family name is everything,' said PG.

'Yes, quite, though not in the way you mean ...'

'My mother killed herself to stop the suspicions and gossip,' he said.

'I think your father believed he'd caught his wife and cousin red-handed, and he was then convinced that the daughter she gave birth to wasn't his.'

'What the hell are you talking about? What daughter?' asked PG.

'Unlike the other branch of the family, your father's side had only ever welcomed sons into the world,' Julia explained.

'Yes, that's correct.'

'Siri always wears her confirmation ring. Werther gave it to her on behalf of the family and said that it belonged to her mother, and he wasn't wrong,' said Julia.

'You've lost me now,' PG sighed.

'In an old film clip we watched, that ring is on your mother's finger, PG. Linnea wore that ring when the King came to visit.'

'But you said ...'

'Just hold on, PG ... You and Werther were sent to Umeå during your mother's pregnancy, and you only came home once Siri had been born. The crying you heard in the corridor wasn't your mother – it was a baby. It was Siri, before she was given away. Sylvester gave his cousin thirty per cent of the company in exchange for adopting her. Your mother couldn't accept the loss of her daughter and took her own life a week later.'

'Oh, God ...'

'The adoption ruined Augustus's marriage, because his wife also believed that the girl was his, which meant she never loved young Siri.'

Siri's chin began to tremble, her face the colour of ash. The rounded diamond on her finger seemed to capture the glow of the chandelier.

'I understand,' she whispered.

'What makes it even more tragic is that Linnea and your father never had any sort of sexual relationship. I started by trying to work out the timings after he shot at the chandelier in the study. It's at least sixty steps from there to the foot of the stairs, and for a man who was blind drunk, well ... you know. If they had been in a compromising position when they heard the shot, they should have been quicker, acted differently, got dressed or climbed out through the window.'

'Speculation,' André sighed.

'Which is supported by Werther's insistence that he called your father over because both PG and Linnea were asleep and he was scared of the dark. Werther and Augustus were playing cards when they heard the gun go off downstairs.'

'But what about before that?' asked Monika. 'Couldn't they have been having an affair anyway?'

'It's possible, of course, but the evening we're talking about – when Sylvester was having dinner with other forestry men – was the first time he'd been away in two months.'

'I understand, but—'

'Siri is your full sister, PG. Werther's too.'

'I'm really struggling to believe any of this,' said PG, pouring himself another whisky.

'It's insane,' Monika agreed.

'In order to be sure, we sent hair samples from both PG and Siri to the National Forensic Centre—'

'What the hell . . . ?'

'And I think Sid has now received the results, but I wanted to share my thinking with you first,' she continued, turning to Sid. 'What does the lab have to say?'

'You want me to look?'

'Please.'

Sid took out his phone and read something with a frown, then looked up at the group.

'They've confirmed it, a hundred per cent match. Siri is your sister, PG.'

# 40

Over by the bar cart, PG knocked back his drink. Siri stared up at Julia and Sid in disbelief. Monika shook her head, a look of scepticism on her face.

'Which takes us back to André,' said Julia. 'You don't seem surprised by any of this.'

'What do you want me to say?'

'You see, the real reason André was able to blackmail Werther so successfully had nothing to do with Björn's injuries,' Julia continued.

'I didn't—'

'You blackmailed Werther,' she cut him off. 'And the reason you were able to do that was because you found Linnea's suicide note.'

'What note?' asked PG. 'There wasn't a note!'

'Yes, there was. And one of the reasons I know this is because during our first conversation, André mentioned that Linnea had struggled to adapt to her role as a woman in this family, as being nothing but a mother. He said it with such confidence, but it made me wonder how he could possibly have known. I hadn't heard anything similar from anyone else, and André was only three when Linnea died.'

'You don't know anything,' André whispered.

'The second link in the chain was the statement we heard before Werther's will: "I once read a letter that stole my soul."'

'Is he the one who found the letter?' asked PG.

'Yes, but somehow it ended up in André's possession. He went to get it from Frida's safe on Sunday afternoon, because he was planning to give it to Werther after the meeting – provided he voted in favour of selling Mannheim.'

'This is bullshit,' said André.

'What clears André of murder also proves he is guilty of blackmail,' said Julia. 'Through Linnea's suicide note, he found out that Siri was Werther and PG's sister, not his. She deserved an equal share to both of them, but he didn't tell Siri any of this – which would have enabled her to demand what was rightfully hers. Instead, André cruelly used this information alongside something else he knew, and contrived to squeeze out shares for himself – hiding behind his brother in case it all went wrong.'

'I don't have to sit here and listen to this crap,' said André, getting to his feet.

'Don't move,' PG growled, slamming his glass down onto the bar cart.

'Yes, you should probably stay,' said Julia.

'Love you too,' André quipped, taking his seat again.

'What does it say in the letter?' asked PG.

'You really want to do this now?'

'We may as well,' said Julia.

André sighed and reached for his bag from the floor. He pulled out a plastic pouch with an envelope inside, took it out and unfolded the letter.

'Should I pass it around, or what?' he asked.

'Just read it,' said Julia.

'Sure?'

'Yes,' said PG.

His face was harried, his lips almost white.

'OK,' said André, putting on his glasses. '"Sylvester. I have accepted that I am worthless, that my life and happiness do not count and that I was simply a vessel for your heirs, but what I do not understand is why I must also be crushed now that my duty is done. Men control reproduction in order to produce sons, who secure their power by controlling reproduction. My life is over. You took my daughter and gave her away. What is left for me now? I can't bear to watch as Werther is robbed of his soul, as he is forced into the mould of the firstborn and made to become part of this cruel, cold, destructive empire. It won't be long until he is just like you, Sylvester, and I hate you more than anyone else on earth. Linnea."'

André took off his glasses and folded the letter around them.

'So, you now understand the cause of the shadows I have been tasked with reading,' Julia said after a moment. 'We have the background, but what really happened to Werther? I'd like to turn to you, Monika, because you were the one who found the email on PG's phone, who marked it as unread and moved it to the junk mail folder. And it was also you and no one else who arranged a meeting with Werther in the brewhouse.'

'I just wanted to talk to him,' Monika whispered.

'She's got a damn alibi,' said PG.

'Yes, we'll come back to that. Monika's plan wasn't to kill Werther, but to talk to him. She knows you would never have the necessary discussion yourself, and so she decided to hide the email from you. Monika has sacrificed everything for her upper-class life here at Mannheim, and—'

'You don't have to sound so disparaging, you know,' said PG.

'That isn't my intention, but I'll explain what I mean in a moment. Monika arranged to meet Werther before the meeting because she wanted to try to convince him not to vote in favour of selling. She borrowed PG's key from his coat pocket, and I know this because Amelie mentioned that she had rust on her hands when she got back from the boat trip.'

'The oarlocks were rusty,' she said, her eyes downcast.

'But I know that it was you, Monika, who was waiting for Werther in the brewhouse. Sadly the meeting didn't go to plan, because just a few minutes later Werther was bleeding on the floor, and not long after that he died.'

Monika's lips were firmly pressed together, her forehead creased in a deep frown.

'Are you telling me it was an accident?' asked PG.

'According to your prenup, Monika doesn't stand to inherit anything in the event of divorce or death,' said Julia, turning to look at everyone again. 'But when the lawyer was here, PG said – in reference to the family's attempts to prevent splitting the property if there were no heirs – that Monika *would* inherit from him ... Which means he must have a will somewhere.'

'It's in our safe,' said PG.

'And if the will was witnessed, then—'

'It was.'

'Then it takes precedence over the prenup,' said Julia. 'Which means that while Monika wouldn't be left with anything in the event of a divorce, she'd inherit *everything* if you died.'

'But I'm not the one who was killed,' he said.

'A valid observation, but not *entirely* true, frighteningly enough,' Julia said with a shudder.

'What do you mean?' PG smiled uncomfortably.

'From our very first meeting in Stockholm, I could sense that you were planning to take your own life if you discovered you were guilty of murder. And you said that your wife was shocked when you showed her the picture.'

'OK . . . ?'

'You also said that she knew you wouldn't be able to live with yourself if it turned out you'd killed another person, and you told me that you would take your punishment if I concluded that you had.'

'Yes.'

'I know you suffer from bipolar disorder, and that you go through periods of deep depression and suicidal thinking.'

'I take my medication.'

'During a later conversation, you said that – like your mother – you would be willing to kill yourself to protect the family name.'

'Of course.'

'PG visits a prostitute in Sundsvall with varying frequency,' said Julia, turning to the others.

'OK, that's enough now.'

'Monika knows about this, because he sends her pictures – of Rosita Navarro, which is the woman's name, while they're taking drugs, having sex ... But those are the exception. Mostly, Rosita provides him with comfort whenever he's struggling.'

'I thought we had a confidentiality clause,' PG pointed out.

'Buying sex and using cocaine and methamphetamine are all against the law. You asked for the full, unadulterated truth,' Julia reminded him.

'OK,' he said with a sigh.

# 41

It felt as though fate itself was present in the Red Room, its gaze shifting between the family members, these lives that were so tangled up in one another. Siri was still sitting perfectly still with big, astonished eyes. Monika looked troubled. André's face was red, and he was sweating. Björn was smiling to himself, and PG suddenly seemed to have aged dramatically.

'But these crimes, the drug taking and procurement of sex, are irrelevant to what I'm trying to explain,' Julia continued after a brief pause. 'The key thing is that Monika knew just how fragile you were, and she knew you would take your own life if you discovered that you'd killed your brother – if not right away then in custody, during the trial or in prison, whenever you entered your next deep depression.'

'Jesus Christ,' Björn whispered.

PG's face was steely as he took in everything Julia had just said.

'You really must hate me,' he said, turning to Monika.

'Everything you've done – the pictures, the humiliation ... I stayed by your side through it all. What else was I meant to do?' she mumbled. 'It broke me, it really did ... You're worse than Werther.'

'That's debatable,' said Julia.

'Yes,' Siri spoke up.

PG rubbed his eyes and slumped down onto the chair by the bar cart.

'Monika believed that if Werther died, PG would inherit everything from him ... and if PG then died too, she would do the same,' Julia continued, pointing to Monika. 'Like PG said earlier, you're the only one with a solid alibi – at least until it crumbled. Monika, you acted with malice, with great cruelty, but you weren't the one who killed Werther ... You arranged to meet him in the brewhouse, even though you'd always been afraid of him.'

'He was a cruel, violent man,' Monika muttered.

'So what were you thinking?'

'That I shouldn't be alone with him.'

'And so you turned to Siri?'

'Yes.'

'Without knowing two key facts about her,' said Julia. 'The two pieces of information André used in his blackmail. The first was that Werther and Siri were siblings, and the second was that they were in a long-term sexual relationship.'

Björn reeled as though someone had just hit him in the face.

'The thought had been lurking at the back of my mind since Sid and I took a taxi back from Sundsvall. As we passed the burnt-out brewhouse, the driver said, "All empires crumble and die eventually ... And the first sign usually goes by the name of Caligula or Cleopatra." He was probably just referring to bad leaders, but Caligula had sex with his sister, and Cleopatra with her brothers.'

Monika and PG turned to Siri. She was sitting tall, but all the colour had drained from her face.

'I've heard a lot of talk about the special relationship Werther and Siri had,' Julia continued. 'She was the only one whose birthday he remembered, and so on. Something clicked when Monika called Siri loose for having the morning after pill in her bag – after all, she wouldn't want to have a child with her brother.'

'This just gets better and better,' said André, knocking back his whisky.

'Plus the fact that Siri identified Werther's body on the basis of the scar on his stomach. A scar he sustained, as we've already mentioned, six years ago. And since no one else recognised it, that made me wonder when Siri could have seen Werther without his shirt on. Just a moment, please ... Now, I'm sure there are other possible explanations for all this, but I'm convinced that their relationship is the reason the murder took place.'

'I don't understand,' said PG, turning to Siri.

'I found the key to what really happened yesterday, after Siri played Chopin on the piano,' Julia went on. 'It was just a brief moment, in the doorway. Monika placed her hand on Siri's cheek. The two of you might not be the best of friends, and you've certainly had your disagreements over the years, but nor are you enemies. The insults and slaps were theatre, to give each other a credible alibi.'

'You don't give an enemy an alibi unless it's true,' said Monika. 'Smart.'

Silence filled the room.

'Siri, it was you who killed Werther,' Julia said quietly.

'No, I—'

All eyes were on her pale, frightened face, her mouth moving silently in an attempt to form words.

'Would you like to tell us what happened?'

'What?' she whispered, looking up.

'Do you want me to do it instead?' Julia asked.

'It was an accident . . .'

'Was it?'

Without warning, tears spilled down Siri's cheeks, over her lips and chin.

'Don't say another word, I'll call a lawyer,' said André, taking out his phone.

'Thank you, but I don't care anymore, I want you to know,' said Siri, taking a deep breath. 'On the day of the AGM, Monika asked me to go to the brewhouse with her. She wanted to talk to Werther, but she was afraid of him.'

Siri swallowed hard and stared at the glass she was still clutching. She put it down and wiped the tears from her face. 'I was hiding behind a secretaire by the workbench, and I heard the conversation spiral out of control almost immediately,' she continued. 'I realise now that Werther must have thought Monika was in on the blackmail with André, because he was furious, screaming that she was a cheap whore, a parasite. "You've got your money, and you won't be getting another fucking penny, you don't understand a thing, I know she's my little sister but I love her, that might make me sick but I—"' Siri trailed off and looked down again.

'And that's where he stopped talking,' said Julia.

Siri opened and closed her mouth several times. A snot bubble burst and ran from her nose.

'I had no idea he was my brother,' she said in a weak voice. 'But he'd known all along ...'

'Yes,' said Julia.

'That's when it all clicked. I realised I'd been groomed, by my own *brother*, that I ... I didn't stand a chance. I was just a kid when it started ... No one else was there for me, Mum hated me and ...'

Her voice broke, and she let out a sob before she composed herself, whispered sorry and dried her cheeks, swallowing several times before she went on.

'I had four miscarriages, and then he started demanding that I took the morning after pill every single time and ...'

She paused again, clamping her hand to her mouth.

Monika got up, marched across the room and wrapped her arms around Siri, rubbing her back and comforting her.

Siri calmed down, blew her nose and then looked up at them all with dark, glittering eyes. Her blonde hair was loose over her slim shoulders, and her cheeks were flushed.

'When I heard Werther say I was his sister, it was like something snapped,' she continued. 'I just grabbed the hammer from the box on the floor, walked over and hit him as hard as I could.'

Her hands were shaking, and the muscles in her jaw tensed.

'Leaving just you and Monika,' Julia said quietly.

'I panicked, I couldn't stop screaming. I couldn't bear to look at him, I was convinced he was going to get up and kill us both,' Siri explained. 'So Monika tied his hands and put a bag over his head ... It was all so crazy ...'

'But you managed to calm down.'

'Monika said she'd fix it. We left the brewhouse, grabbed the coffee and buns, locked the door and then went out onto the lake.'

'What did Monika say? You'd formed an unholy alliance, hadn't you?' asked Julia.

'She told me about PG, the way he humiliated her, the prenup. And she said she was willing to protect me if I helped make sure he took the fall ...'

'Yes.'

Siri turned to PG, who was still sitting by the bar cart.

'I'm sorry,' she said. 'I didn't know the rest of it, that she was hoping you'd kill yourself.'

He stared back at her with glassy eyes. His face was stony, harried, the lines like deep, dark brushstrokes.

'The two of you decided that you, Siri, would get hold of PG's phone just before midnight. You'd take a picture of the body and then put the phone back, and then you would act like you were in an escalating argument,' said Julia. 'Monika would make sure PG got drunk and drugged up, and she'd lure him out to the brewhouse. She also poured port onto the rug in the Red Room and asked Amelie for help, in order to give herself both an alibi and a fellow witness to seeing PG out in the dark. You were hoping PG would go into the brewhouse and get blood all over himself, but even if he didn't, the photograph on his phone would be entirely in line with his habit of documenting his sins.'

'Yes,' Siri whispered.

'PG didn't go into the brewhouse that evening, and he didn't call the police. But the next morning, once he'd seen the photograph, he drove straight to Stockholm and hired us, which made Monika nervous. She then dragged the body down to the water, well aware that the current would carry it down to the dam, where it would be found after a few days.'

'We decided that anyone who did that must want the body to be found,' said Sidney.

'Most killers would go to great lengths to hide the body and wash the blood from their hands, but Monika's plan hinged on making sure there was a police investigation,' Julia explained. 'Werther's body had to be found, and she also knew she would have to destroy any evidence implicating herself and Siri in the brewhouse. We initially thought that our arrival had put pressure on the killer and forced them into starting the fire, but that night was probably just the first opportunity she got.'

'You're right,' Monika whispered, without looking up.

'Everyone hated Werther, even Werther himself,' said Julia, bracing herself against her cane. 'I once read a letter that stole my soul, that was what he wrote to you all ... and perhaps that is true. Werther was only fifteen when his mother died, writing in her suicide note that he was turning into his father, oppressing those around him and hated by his mother. He spent his entire adolescence knowing that he would one day take over from his father, and suddenly he knew exactly how that would happen, what his role in the family would be. As a result, he became a tyrant, tormenting the rest of you children and exploiting his sister ...'

'Which also made us the people we are today,' said PG.

'Werther transferred ten per cent of the shares and was prepared to sell Mannheim in exchange for the letter,' Julia explained. 'At first, that seemed to be out of greed, but in actual fact he did it to protect his sister from the truth. By leaving her his remaining twenty-five per cent in his will, she would end up with a greater share than she would have been entitled to as a rightful heir.'

'But that will no longer be the case, thanks to the paragraph one, chapter fifteen of the inheritance code,' said Sid. 'It's down to the courts, obviously, but murder is generally a pretty powerful reason to deviate from the typical order of inheritance.'

'Werther left everything to Siri, possibly in an attempt to make amends, but by a twist of fate she ended up killing him,' said Julia. 'Which, I think, is a reminder that a person simply can't buy their way out of certain deeds.'

'No,' Siri whispered.

A silence swept in over the grand halls of Mannheim like some sort of slow-moving shockwave of uncovered secrets and naked truths.

People often talk about an angel walking through a room, but on this occasion it was Julia's faultless logic that struck them.

'Pretty bloody impressive,' said Björn, slowly clapping his hands.

'Seriously, who are you?' André asked.

'Stark Detective Agency,' Julia replied, tapping her cane on the floor three times.

'The police and prosecution agency will take over now,' said Sid.

PG cleared his throat. 'I know I asked for the truth, but I'm really questioning whether it was all worth it now.'

'If we hadn't got to the bottom of this, you would have taken your own life as a result of a lie . . . just like your mother,' said Julia.

Siri looked up for the first time in some while, her eyes now remarkably steely. 'I'm glad I killed Werther,' she said quietly. 'I wouldn't hesitate to do it all again.'

# Epilogue

On 24 August, Julia and Sid were sitting at a table at the Ekstedt restaurant in central Stockholm. The room was buzzing, and the glow of the open fire pulsed like light bouncing off water over the guests' faces in the dimly lit space.

Julia had been planning to offer Sid a trial position at the detective agency that evening, but every time a gap opened up in the conversation she got so nervous that she could hear her blood roaring in her ears.

They had just finished their starter of smoked mussels, halibut and samphire, and as soon as the waiting staff had cleared away their plates, they toasted and continued their conversation about the Mannheim case.

The prosecutor had now taken over the preliminary investigation and remanded both Monika and Siri in custody. PG had admitted to procuring sex, and André and Björn were being investigated for blackmail and insurance fraud.

Julia and Sid stopped talking as the waitress set down a red hot cast-iron dish on their table, serving each of them a small taco of elk heart and lingonberries in sizzling butter.

As they ate, Julia grew serious, talking about the mistake she had made by pointing the finger at Björn.

'The police officers gave me a telling-off like I was some kid who'd prank called the emergency services,' she sighed.

'You shouldn't be too hard on yourself,' said Sid, wiping a little burnt butter from his lips.

'I'm just such an idiot sometimes ...'

'You were great, you solved the case.'

She looked deep into his eyes and had to stop herself from reaching out to touch his hand.

'With your help,' she said.

'I'm serious though, you were incredible ... That speech in the library.'

'You got me to think logically at the last minute, that's the effect you have on me. You stop me getting carried away as soon as I find a couple of pieces that fit together. That's precisely the kind of help I need.'

'Well, I'm glad I could be of use.'

Julia looked down, trying to compose herself though her heart was racing faster than ever. Though her hands were shaking so much she barely dared lift her wine glass to her mouth.

'You really were,' she said, swallowing hard. 'But also ... you know ...'

'Don't be sad,' he said quietly.

She blinked away the tears and forced herself to meet his eye. 'Do you think you'd ever consider ... having dinner with me again? Every now and then, I mean, nothing more than that ...'

'I'd love to,' he said, placing his rough hand on hers.

His touch flooded through her, making her heart flutter and her cheeks grow hot.

'You don't have to if you don't want to ...'

'But I do.'

'Oh, there was one more thing ... What if I need more professional help?'

'We'll see ...'

Julia's phone pinged in her bag, and she whispered an apology, took it out and read the message. She was powerless to stop a slight smile from creeping onto her face.

'Have you heard of Bianca Salo, the actress?' she asked.

'Of course. I saw her as Puck in *A Midsummer Night's Dream* last spring. Why?'

'She wants to hire Stark Detective Agency.'

'Did she say why?'

'She says her dead fiancé is stalking her.'